Mercer's face contorted. His shoulder dipped, and he started his grab for the gun. He wasn't good, and the men he had killed must have been remarkably bad. A smooth draw was as fluid as flowing water, and Mercer didn't have it.

Rush waited until Mercer's hand touched the gun butt before he drew. . . .

GILES A. LUTZ is the author
of the following Ace books:

THE
DEMANDING
LAND

by

GILES A. LUTZ

ace books
A Division of Charter Communications Inc.
1120 Avenue of the Americas
New York, N.Y. 10036

I

Rush Sawyer thought bleakly, *It sure as hell spread fast.* People gawked at him from doors and windows as he rode down Main Street. It didn't surprise him. From the moment Johnny Larson had spotted him a couple of miles out of town, then wheeled and galloped like a hot-assed Indian, Rush knew this kind of reception would be waiting for him.

He thought with sour humor that he must have been pretty famous around here three years ago. This curiosity was a natural aftermath.

He kept his eyes straight ahead. He knew most of these staring people, and they knew him. But so far he hadn't heard a word of greeting. *Welcome home, Rush Sawyer,* he thought, and he couldn't keep the rancor out of it. People were quick to kick, when they thought they had somebody down, but damnit, didn't they ever quit kicking? A twinge of unease ran through him. Maybe all his reports were false; maybe he wasn't as free to ride down this street as he thought.

5

Naw, he thought. He had checked out everything as best he could. He hadn't let his eagerness to come home turn him foolish. Old Ben Cavanaugh had long claws. Rush made sure he had them out of him before he ever turned the gelding's nose in this direction. Still, he'd better clear everything at the sheriff's office. He grinned frostily. Sam Tabor wasn't going to be overjoyed to see him, either.

He dismounted before the sheriff's office, wrapped his reins, and stood thoughtfully for a moment. He was a man of average height, and the lean face was stamped with a bone weariness. Both man and horse showed the long, wearing miles between Mexico and Oregon.

He slapped halfheartedly at the dust in his clothes, then let it go. He knew every inch of this town, and yet it seemed strange to him. He guessed he wouldn't really feel home until he saw the ranch again.

He thought, *You're just putting off seeing Sam,* and grinned. The harsh severity left his face when he grinned, and the mouth was mobile with humor. He had deep-set dark eyes in a rough-carved face, and the black hair was inclined to string down across his forehead. Slim riders' legs carried a horseman's torso, with his main weight concentrated in the heavy chest, back, and arm muscles. His hands were work-scarred and competent-looking. He was twenty-four years old, but when his face was in repose, he looked ten years older.

He said, "Let's get it over with," and strode toward the door.

He stepped inside and after the brilliance of the sunshine squinted against the shadowy interior. This office hadn't changed. He could swear the same *wanted* posters were on the walls, perhaps a little more yellowed with age. The floor was still tobacco-stained and mud-lumped. The same sour smell of urine pails and of bedding, too infrequently washed, came from the three cells at the end of the office. He would never forget that smell. Two weeks in one of those cells ground that smell into a man's nose forever.

Sam Tabor sat in the same creaky swivel chair behind the

desk, his legs extended, his bootheels hooked on the desk's edge. His hat was pulled down over his eyes, and his hands were folded across his stomach. A casual observer would say he was asleep, but Rush knew he wasn't. Tabor's body wasn't relaxed. Rush would bet Tabor saw him the moment he threw off in front of the office.

"Hello, Sam," he drawled.

Tabor thumbed the hatbrim out of his eyes and his bootheels thumped against the floor. His face looked like an arctic winter as he stared at Rush.

"I thought you'd turn up," he growled.

His cheeks were hollowed, and his complexion had a gray tinge. Age had deteriorated him to a certain point, then seemed to lose its force. Three years hadn't changed him much. Maybe the lines were deeper in his face and his shoulders stooped more. But that was all.

"You got anything against me?" Rush asked.

Tabor's eyes smoldered. "Shouldn't I have? You split my head." His hand unconsciously rose toward the back of his head. Rush must have hit him an awful lick for Tabor to retain the instinctive memory this long. "You broke jail. And you walk in here and ask me, if I got anything against you."

The night Tabor spoke of was vivid in Rush's memory. A twenty-one year old can get pretty scared and frantic. The town was howling for his scalp, and Ben Cavanaugh was howling the loudest. He had put on a convincing act. The fake bellyache doubled him over and put him to twisting and bumping over the cell floor. Tabor had entered with drawn gun and bent over him. Rush could still recall the sound of Tabor's startled squawk, when a hand fastened on the gun and wrenched it out of his hand. Rush didn't have the time or inclination to figure out the degree of force to use. He had just struck with the gun barrel, and Tabor had slumped to the floor.

"What the hell did you expect?" Rush asked savagely. "What would you have done, if you had the Cavanaughs snapping at your heels, if you felt a rope getting tighter around your neck every day?"

7

A faint grin tugged at Tabor's lip corners before he controlled it. "Maybe I'd have done the same. You stole Neilson's horse, too."

"I did not," Rush denied hotly. "I sent him the money for it. I paid him more than it was worth.

"A year later," Tabor acknowledged sourly.

"Goddamnit. I had to find work."

Tabor nodded. "I suppose. He showed me your letter. I got the postmark and wrote to that town, asking the law to pick you up. I'd have been pretty happy to get my hands on you. Where did you go?"

"I figured my letter would put you back on my tail. I slipped over the line into Mexico."

"I guessed it," Tabor grunted. "And now you're back."

Tabor sounded as though he had no right to be.

"Hell," Rush protested. "There can't be a charge against me. Clayton confessed he killed Dan Cavanaugh." An edge of anxiety was in his voice. "I wrote Doc Somers and checked it with him."

"Clayton confessed all right. He died hard. That horse busted him up real good. Doc and I were with him just before he died. There was bad blood between him and Dan over Flora Belle." His face was reflective. "I was glad, when that floozie left town. She caused a lot of trouble. Dan was a handy man with his fists." That frosty grin touched his mouth again. "You oughta remember that. You were the only man I knew who ever whipped him."

"He damned near killed me that night," Rush admitted. They had fought for twenty minutes, and everybody at the dance had watched them. That had been over a girl, too. It looked as though Dan Cavanaugh had collected all the women he could and fought to keep them.

"I barely had enough left to stagger off before I passed out," Rush said. "The next thing I knew you were arresting me for Dan's murder."

"It looked like it," Tabor said. "Dan was found an hour later with his head bashed in. You didn't have any reason to love him."

8

"I tried to tell you I didn't have anything to do with it," Rush said bitterly. "But nobody listened to me."

"Ben Cavanaugh's got a big voice," Tabor said quietly. "When he's shouting, nobody can hear much else. Clayton had a lot of mad to work off on Dan. Dan had whipped him a couple of times over Flora Belle. Clayton laid for him and busted his head with a rock. After your fight with Dan he figured everybody would be looking for you. He sure as hell was right. You oughta be grateful to him. You'd still be tagged, if he hadn't talked before he died."

Rush could find no gratitude for Clayton. Who was going to pay for those lonely years in exile? So far, nobody had even said they were sorry for the mistake.

He asked, "Am I square with everybody?"

Tabor nodded. "You're square. What are you going to do now?"

That wasn't just friendly curiosity in Tabor's voice. He had a definite reason for wanting to know.

"I'm going home," Rush said flatly. "And give Paw whatever help I can."

The hard inquisitiveness left Tabor's eyes. "He needs it, Rush. He's been going downhill ever since your Maw died. I'm real sorry about that."

Rush's eyes were bleak. His mother died the first year he was away. He hadn't heard about it until six months ago. Letters had a hard time catching up with a man on the move from the law.

He said a grim, "Yes," in acknowledgment of Tabor's sympathy.

"You're not holding any grudge?" Tabor persisted.

Rush frowned. Who could he hold a grudge against? Clayton was dead. Tabor and all the others had acted as they saw it. Looking back, Rush could see how neatly everything fitted. No, it was all a bad break, and moaning over it wouldn't do a damned bit of good.

"No grudges," he said. It was odd that Tabor was worried about that. "I just want to settle down again."

"Ben Cavanaugh doesn't feel that way," Tabor said softly. "Neither does Odie."

Odie Cavanaugh was Ben's youngest son. He was four years younger than Rush, and he looked like a replica of his dead brother. He had Dan's size and the same pushy, belligerent nature. With the Cavanaugh's money behind him all his life, he hadn't learned much real value.

For a moment Rush didn't understand what Tabor meant. "But you said—" he started bewilderedly.

Tabor nodded. "I said Clayton confessed. And it was the truth. I believed him. But Ben Cavanaugh didn't. You know Ben. Once he gets an idea in his head dynamite won't blast it out. He spent every minute of three years thinking about you. He built up a powerful hate. He's not going to let go of it easy."

Rush felt a momentary helplessness, then his anger wiped it away. "What are you trying to tell me?"

"Stay clear of the Cavanaughs," Tabor said flatly. "Don't go out of your way to irritate Ben. Give this time to die down."

Rush's eyes blazed. "Are you telling me to bow and scrape before him? Beg him for the right to live around here? Go to hell, Sam."

He stalked toward the door. He turned there for a final remark. "I'll mind my own business, Sam. But nobody is pushing on me."

He stepped out onto the walk.

Tabor sighed. He was afraid Rush would take it that way. He couldn't blame Rush. And he could see how Ben Cavanaugh felt, too. Ben had set a store in Dan. And he was a stubborn man. It would take him time to reverse his thinking. Tabor's face was gloomy. A man didn't have to have the ability to see into the future to know there was trouble ahead.

II

RUSH'S FACE was set in a scowl as he moved toward the hitchrack. He was clean with the law, but it was a different matter with the Cavanaughs. The Cavanaughs never forgot or forgave a real or fancied hurt. And he had fought and whipped Dan. That alone was enough to harden in Ben Cavanaugh's head. And Odie would break his back, trying to please his father. Rush had no intention of crossing their paths. He only wished they felt the same about him.

He rolled and lit a cigarette before he reached out to unwrap his reins. Spring was here, but the breeze was still chilly. He shivered involuntarily. His light jacket, that was more than adequate in the warm southern country, wasn't enough here.

His sojourn in Texas and Mexico had thinned his blood. But then, any season in the Owyhee could be rough on a man. Nature hadn't been kind to this region. The stunted, struggling trees were proof of that as was the sparse grass. Rainfall was meager, and the soil was thin and rocky. It took thirty acres to support a cow, and a man could sum up this country by saying, it was rimrock, sagebrush and badger holes.

The town showed the struggle it took to exist here. The buildings had a wind-scrubbed look, and few of them had any paint left. Every country had some disadvantage, but this one had them all. Rush wondered why people persisted in living here. Home, he supposed. A man's roots went down deep in the country where he was born.

He flipped the half-smoked cigarette away and unwrapped his reins. He was lifting his boot toward the stirrup, when a voice from across the street, hailed him.

11

"Rush, you mangy, ole coyote."

He grinned and turned his head. Only his friends would hail him like that.

Jim Yates raced across the street. He threw his arms around Rush, then mauled him. For a moment, the delight of their greeting was as rough as a fight. Then Yates' face sobered as he seized Rush's hand and wrung it.

"I'm glad you're back," he said. "I figured you'd hear someway and be drifting in one of these days. I didn't know where to write you."

"If you could write," Rush jeered to cover his emotion.

He had a powerful lot of feeling for this man. They had grown up together, for the Yates had the ranch next to Mundro Sawyer's. They had worked and played and drank together. A couple of times they had fought each other over some disagreement. But when the fight was over, the disagreement was gone. Yates was long and stringy. He was a year older than Rush, but his weather-worn face looked far older. The struggle of making a living was written in the toughened skin, in the squint lines around his eyes, in the lean, hungry-looking stretch of him. He was tough and competent, a good man to have for a friend.

They dropped hands suddenly as they realized the excess of emotion they had displayed.

"How's Mundro?" Rush asked.

"He's looking down the road every day for you," Yates answered. He shook his head, a gesture that was more expressive than words. "He's gone downhill, Rush, since your maw died."

Tabor had said the same thing. Rush felt something twist inside him. "Yes," he said quietly. He knew what Alice Sawyer had meant to his father. The harsh knotting of anger twisted his guts. The Cavanaughs couldn't be blamed for his mother's death, but they had forced him to flee, and his being away hadn't helped any.

"Did he have trouble with the Cavanaughs?"

"Everybody has trouble with them," Yates growled. "They plagued him every little way they could."

12

Rush swore silently. By God, that was going to be changed as of right now.

He said, "I'll see you later, Jim."

"You can't go without me buying you a drink," Yates protested. "Then I'll ride out with you."

Rush didn't want the drink, but he hated to turn Yates down. "One," he said. "No more."

"No more," Yates promised.

Rush rewrapped the reins and crossed the street diagonally with Yates toward the Case Ace. He remembered the saloon well, particularly the night he and Yates had tried to take it apart. Sam Tabor had put a quick stop to that. Lud Wakeman remembered the night, too. His face always got tight after that, whenever Yates and Rush walked into his place.

He grinned as he asked, "Do you think Lud will be glad to see me?"

"If he is, he'll be the only one," Yates answered.

Wakeman looked up as they entered the saloon. That old, tight look was on his face. He was a pudgy, little man with the harassed face of the worrier. But he ran an honest place and served the best whisky he could, for the price.

Hell, Rush thought. *We didn't do that much damage for that look to last this long.*

He saw Wakeman swing his eyes to the middle of the bar. Ben and Odie Cavanaugh stood there, their backs toward him. Wakeman's look wasn't hard to understand now. He was scared to death of another fight in here.

Yates said in a low voice, "We can go on down the street." His eyes danced as he saw the old, familiar stubbornness harden Rush's face.

"I didn't think you'd want to."

"No," Rush said shortly. He wasn't going to start out by ducking the Cavanaughs. That quickly grew to be habit forming until a man was running all the time.

He could have stopped at this end of the bar, leaving a wide space between himself and the Cavanaughs, but perversely, he chose the far end. And he would make no pretense of steering a wide course around them.

The Cavanaughs must have picked up his reflection in the back mirror, for they swung around and faced him.

Ben Cavanaugh said, "This goddamned town is going to pieces. They let anything walk its streets."

All of the Cavanaughs were big men, but the years were beginning to lard Ben's frame. His belt was losing its battle to restrain his belly, and his jowls were as heavy as a hog's. A grizzled look was beginning to sprinkle his red hair, and his face had a raw, reddish, beefy look. He was the big man in this country, and men paid him respect, even though unwillingly. He had carved a successful ranch out of this stingy country, and that alone entitled him to standing.

Odie Cavanaugh was a younger edition of his father. He had the same beefy look, the same florid complexion that burned instead of tanning. His eyes were small and pinched tight together, and the wide mouth was loose-lipped. He was twenty years old, and he had worshiped Dan.

His grin displayed a toothless gap. "Even jailbirds," he said.

He worked hard to win Ben's approval, but he'd never be the man Dan had been.

Rush threw a warning look at Yates. The look said, *Ignore it.*

He was on the inside, and he passed within a couple of feet of the Cavanaughs.

Odie thrust his foot out suddenly, and the tripping sent Rush pitching forward. He lit on his shoulder, and the impact was hard enough to snap his head forward. His cheekbone slammed into the floor. It put a roaring into his head, and a fluid blackness danced before his eyes. His mouth filled with a heavy stickiness, and it took him a moment to realize he must have bitten his tongue.

"He's a clumsy bastard," Odie said, and his voice seemed to come from a long distance off.

Rush lay there, waiting for his scattered senses to regroup and return to him.

He pushed to his hands and knees and shook his head vi-

14

olently. The blackness was fading, and the roaring in his head was lessening. His cheek stung, and he supposed the rough flooring had scraped it raw.

He lifted his head at Wakeman's frantic cry. "No, Rush, no. It was just an accident."

Ben Cavanaugh had a tight, frozen smile on his face, and Odie wore a broad grin. Yates stood just beyond them, and his face was carved out of marble, but there was anger in his eyes, a blazing anger.

Rush pushed to his feet, and his knee hinges weren't steady. A jar like that took a lot out of a man. His stomach was still swinging around as though it had lost its anchoring, and he squinted against the watering in his eyes.

He spat into the sawdust and saw the red-tinged blob roll and gather bulk. "Don't get in this, Jim," he said.

"Was it an accident, Odie?" he asked. His face looked mournful, almost pleading.

Both of the Cavanaughs misread him. There was no menace in his posture, and the eyes weren't savage.

"You'd better take it that way," Ben Cavanaugh said. "You'd better grab your out."

"Maybe you're right, Ben," Rush said mildly and started to move past them. Out of the corner of his eye he caught the shock, molding Yates' features. Rush Sawyer had never taken something like this in his life.

He pivoted suddenly, changing the direction of his next stride. It carried him into Odie, and Odie was a damned fool. He was still draped over the edge of the bar, all relaxed and easy.

Rush poured a right hand into Odie's belly, and he saw the eyes bulge with hurt and surprise. An explosive burst of breath fanned his face.

Wakeman yelled, "Stop it," then Rush heard the pound of his running feet. Wakeman was after somebody who could stop it.

Yates snapped, "Touch that gun, Ben, and I'll blow your goddamned head off."

Rush watched Odie with wicked interest in his eyes. Odie

15

looked sick. The florid hue had disappeared from his face, and it was now a pasty color tinged with green. His meaty lips kept opening in soundless gags, and he had his arms held tight against his belly. He tried to straighten up, but the hurt in his middle kept him bent over.

"Don't get mad, Odie," Rush said. "It was only an accident."

He slammed a fist at the exposed jaw, and it rode in a little high. It landed on the cheekbone, and it helped Odie straighten up. It jerked his head back and put a glaze in his eyes.

Ben Cavanaugh must have made a move, for Rush heard Yates say, "Go ahead, Ben. Just give me an excuse."

Ben Cavanaugh's voice was thick and garbled with anger. "Goddammn it. Give him a chance."

"Like the tripping he gave Rush," Yates said mockingly. "I hope he cuts him to ribbons."

Odie made feeble, pawing motions, and his eyes weren't focusing well. He had vitality. He had taken two hard blows, but he was still on his feet.

Rush was tempted to cut him to ribbons. It wouldn't have been hard. That face was completely unprotected. He pushed the temptation aside as he cocked his fist. He got the solid weight of his shoulder behind the blow and felt the shock of the impact run the length of his arm and smash into his shoulder.

It was a wicked blow. It landed on Odie's jaw hinge and rolled his eyes up into his head. He made a bubbling, wet noise as he straightened, and for a moment Rush thought he wasn't going down. Then he saw the knees begin to bend, and Odie was falling.

Rush stepped to one side and locked his hands together. As Odie's fall carried him past Rush, he swung the locked hands in a brutal arcing swing toward the exposed neck. Rush felt the edge of his palms dig into the beefy neck and grunted with effort and satisfaction. If that blow on the jaw left Odie anything, this vicious chop to the neck would wipe it away.

16

Odie hit the floor and bounced. He came back down with a flat, sprawling inertness, and he didn't even twitch.

Rush's right hand hurt. He saw the depression where his right knuckle should be and sucked on it. He took the hand from his mouth and looked at Yates. "Damnit," he said plaintively. "I knocked a knuckle down."

"You should've known better than to use your hands on a Cavanaugh head," Yates said reprovingly. His face had a happy grin.

Ben Cavanaugh looked as though he were in the grip of a stroke. His face was purplish, and his mouth kept opening and closing as he grabbed for air.

"You killed him," he screeched.

Yates looked down at Odie. He could see the irregular movement in Odie's back as he breathed. "No," he said regretfully. "Rush doesn't have that much luck."

Cavanaugh was in the grip of an insane fury, and ordinary caution might be lost to him. Yates said, "Unbuckle that gunbelt, Ben. And do it damned easy."

Cavanaugh looked at him as though he didn't understand, and Rush watched him with worried eyes. Surely, Ben wasn't crazy enough to go for his gun. If he did, Yates would shoot him, and Rush didn't want him pulled into this.

He said evenly, "Better do as he says, Ben."

It wiped away some of the wildness in Ben's eyes, and his fingers moved carefully to the belt buckle and undid it. He let the belt fall, and it thumped against the floor.

Rush had never seen more hating in a man's face.

"This isn't over yet," Ben said thickly.

Rush heard the pound of running feet and turned his head toward the door. Tabor burst through it, and Wakeman was on his heels. Wakeman had found Tabor in a hurry.

"Stop them, Sam," he squalled. "Before they wreck my place. Before—" His words tailed off as he looked around with confused eyes. Everything was intact.

17

Tabor's face was furious. "What the hell's going on here?" he roared.

"Arrest him," Ben Cavanaugh yelled. "He jumped Odie, when Odie wasn't looking. Look at Odie. He almost killed him."

"Tell it straight," Yates said savagely. "Lud, tell him how it happened." His eyes bored through Wakeman.

Wakeman looked like a rabbity, little man, but he had a certain amount of courage. He couldn't quite meet Ben's eyes as he said, "Odie started it. Rush and Jim were moving by them, when Odie tripped Rush. He went down hard."

Tabor looked at Rush's skinned cheek. "That it, Rush?"

"That's it," Rush said curtly.

"You didn't say anything to him?"

"Ben and Odie did all the talking," Wakeman said. "Odie called Rush a jailbird. Rush still didn't say anything."

Tabor's rage exploded. "Damn you, Ben. I talked to you and told you it was over. You can't get anything through your thick head, can you? If you keep pushing on this—" His words were coming too fast, and he stopped and breathed hard.

"I won't warn you again," he said in a quieter voice. "Lud, get me some water."

Wakeman went behind the bar and came back with a gallon fruit can, filled with water. His hands were shaking, and he spilled some of it as he handed it to Tabor.

Tabor towed Odie over and dumped the can into his face. The water soaked Odie's head and jacketfront, and he sputtered and spit. His eyes flew open, and he stared around vaguely.

"Hey," Yates said in delight. "We didn't think of drowning him."

Tabor glared at him, then looked at Ben Cavanaugh. "Get him out of here," he ordered.

Ben tried to help Odie to his feet, and he couldn't make it.

Tabor reached down, grabbed Odie by the collar, and helped Ben haul him erect.

He propped Odie against the bar and asked, "Odie, can you understand me?"

Odie was still sputtering, but his eyes weren't quite as vague.

"Odie," Tabor said. "I won't let you off this easy next time. I figured you collected plenty for this. But make me more trouble and see what happens."

Ben Cavanaugh was trying to recall his shredded dignity. The rage was still in his eyes, but it was a different rage. This one was cold and thinking.

"Can I have my gun?" he asked.

"Pick it up," Tabor ordered.

Ben buckled on the belt. "Sam, I won't forget this. You used to be able to count on my support. You can't any more. I won't forget this."

"Get out of here," Tabor yelled.

He watched Cavanaugh stagger toward the door under Odie's weight.

When the doors swung to again, he faced Rush. "I knew you'd be back," he said gloomily. "And I knew you'd bring trouble."

"What the hell did you expect him to do?" Yates exploded. "Just take that tripping and apologize to them for living?"

"Hold it, Jim," Rush said. Everybody involved had a different point of view. He was grateful to Tabor for one thing. Tabor had listened and then made a fair judgment. He hadn't jumped on the Cavanaughs' side merely because they were Cavanaughs. It could've happened.

He said, "I need that drink now, Jim. Join us, Sam? Jim's buying."

Tabor shook his head wearily. "Too early." An unconscious note of pleading was in his voice. "Rush, all I'm asking is that you don't go out of your way to rile them."

"You can depend on that, Sam." He added a mental, *If they'll let me.*

Tabor looked at him with gloomy eyes. "I hope so, Rush."

III

RUSH AND YATES rode out of town and stopped at the first
bend in the Snake. The river ran low and sullen-looking. It
looked harmless enough now, but Rush had seen it in flood.
Then it became a mighty force, sweeping everything before
it. He looked at the muddy-brown water. Its low level meant
only one thing: insufficient rainfall. He'd take the flooding
anytime. It was rough on the people who lived along the
river, but it meant that the interior got moisture.

He said, "No rain again this spring, Jim?"

Yates swore passionately. He damned nature and its par-
simoniousness. He said, "It seems like she sets herself up
to devil a man every way she can. If she's not giving too
much, it's too little. The only thing she seems to favor is
rattlesnakes and sagebrush. How come she's such a goddamned tramp, Rush?"

Rush smiled in sympathy. He had voiced those same curses
against the same subject many times. He had heard preachers
speak of how grateful man should be to a benevolent nature. He hadn't seen that side of her face at all. He would
say she was a tight-fisted, stingy bitch.

He swung down and walked to the water's edge. The
skinned side of his face felt dried and stiff, and he bathed
it tenderly. He dipped his hand into the water and felt
a momentary easing in the thumping of the abused knuckle.

He raised his hand and looked at it. The damned hand
was swelling.

Yates grinned and said, "Think of how marked up you'd
be if he'd had fought back."

His eyes went wide in alarm as Rush's hand flashed
toward his gun.

The rattlesnake lay not two feet in back and to the side of Yates, its protective coloring blending with the ground. The spring sun didn't yet have enough warmth to drive the torpor out of it, but it was beginning to lift its head, and its tongue was darting. It was coiled, and Rush didn't know how long it was. But its strike could have enough length to reach Yates. Rush didn't dare yell a warning. Yates' frightened jump could carry him closer to the snake.

Rush felt the stab of protest from his injured knuckle as his hand closed around the gun, but the draw was still fast and fluid. He fired without apparent aiming, and the bullet tore through the S-shaped coils.

Yates whipped his head around and looked at the floppings of the dying snake.

He said, "Jesus," and his face was loose. He rubbed the back of his hand across his forehead, and there was a shakiness in the gesture.

"For a second, I thought you'd gone crazy," he said. "I thought you were pulling on me." He looked at the pistol in Rush's hand. "It looks like you learned something since you've been gone."

Rush put the gun away. "A little," he said dryly. That old Texan had taught him well. Rush had never been able to separate fact from legend about the man, but there was no doubt he had been one of the names among the gunfighters. The man was old, when Rush knew him, and his hands were crippled with rheumatism. He couldn't show Rush how to do it, but he could tell him. And Rush had drawn and aimed and fired ten million times before the Texan was satisfied.

"You're good," the Texan had finally said. "But don't go looking for chances to prove it. Use it only when you have to."

Rush had never forgotten that advice. He had used the skill on a tequila-crazed native in Mexico, who came at him with a knife, and a couple of other times on snakes. But those had been necessities.

Yates had a reflective look in his eyes. "Maybe a lot

21

of us will be glad you've got it before everything's over."

Rush shook his head. The gesture said many things.

The snake was still quivering when Yates put his boot-heel on its head and ground it into the soil. "I hate the goddamned things." He hadn't said a word of thanks. He didn't have to.

They remounted and rode in silence, each man occupied with his own thoughts. Yates broke it by pointing to a bunch of distant dots on a high point. "The Oreanas," he said.

Rush had caught them a second before Yates spoke. Eastern Oregon abounded in the wild horses, the slick-ears, or the broomtails as most called them. They were said to be descended from the original Spanish horses, either strayed, abandoned, or stolen by Indians from the conquistadores. They knew neither men, bridles, or branding irons. Through the years they had crossed with runaway saddlehorses and work stock, and they were small and inbred. They weighed on an average of six to eight hundred pounds, and the ordinary cowboy scorned them. What there was of them was built pretty strong, and their hooves were as hard as the rocks they ran on. Cattlemen hated them, for they competed with the cattle for the short forage. They had remarkable wind and endurance. Rush had chased and roped them for fun, and some of them had wild, matted manes as heavy as a bundle of straw on their necks, and the tails were so long they dragged the ground. Every color of the rainbow was among them: blue and strawberry roans, pintos, canellos, and sevinas. Rush had even seen a few byos, the buckskins striped black on their backs, legs and withers, like a zebra.

"Damned worthless things," Yates grumbled. "Rattlesnakes and oreanas. That's about all that can live here."

Rush grinned at him. It was too bad the wild horses weren't worth something. There were enough of them.

"Goddamned country," Yates muttered and lapsed into silence.

The miles dropped behind them, and neither man spoke until they reached the turnoff to the Sawyer Ranch. The

22

buildings lay a mile down that rutted lane, and Rush asked, "Come in for a cup of coffee?"

Yates shook his head with elaborate casualness. "Got to be getting home. I'll see you later."

Rush smiled faintly as he watched Yates ride on. Yates had keen perception. He wanted to give Rush those first few moments alone with Mundro.

It was odd how coming home put a tightness in a man's chest. He couldn't see the house and outbuildings until he crested that last small rise, then they were suddenly thrown out before him in that little bowl.

He frowned at them. He didn't remember them as being so run-down looking. They had a tired list, and he saw too many missing boards. This was a hardscrabble ranch, and he eased off on the criticism. He guessed Mundro had been too busy making a living to find time for repairs. *It's always looked like this,* he thought. *You've been away long enough for it to hit you in the face.* This hard, demanding country kept a man running just to stay in place, and that wasn't always successful. Each year the bank took a little deeper bite on the land. If a man could just get hold of a decent sum of money, he could make his repairs and put the place back into shape. He let go of that fancy illusion. How was a man going to get hold of a sum like that, when it took all of his energies just to make a living. That last, long hill was always before the little man, and it seem that none of them ever made it.

He lifted the reins and said, "Let's go, boy. I promise you, you won't move a hoof for a month, unless you want to."

He saw a figure come out onto the porch and a hand lift to shade eyes as it peered toward him. Yates had said Mundro looked down the road every day. More likely, he had heard the sound of hooves.

Mundro Sawyer stepped out into the yard to meet his son. He was a small, bandy-legged man, and the years rode his shoulders hard. His hair was thinning and graying, and the wrinkles in his face looked like erosion furrows caused by rushing water. The thing that upset Rush the most was that his eyes were dead. That was real bad, for when that happened to a man, it didn't take too long for the rest of him to start dying too.

He said, "Hello, Mundro," and swung down.

"Rush," Mundro said and reached out a hand.

Rush felt the trembling in it, and Mundro's eyes were all squinty.

They let the pressure of their hands say what they felt.

"Been quite a spell," Mundro said, and his voice had an unnatural huskiness.

"Long enough," Rush said flatly. To keep the moment from growing more solemn he said, "I'll bet you let the work pile up for me."

"I did pretty fair at it," Mundro said dryly. "You come through town?"

"I talked to Tabor. I'm clear with him." He didn't intend to say a word about the Cavanaughs. There was no need to pile unnecessary worry on Mundro's shoulders.

"But not the Cavanaughs." Munro made it a statement instead of a question, and Rush's eyes sharpened.

"What made you say that?" he demanded.

Mundro made an aimless gesture with his hand. "You know Ben. It's hard for him to accept things."

"Has he been making you trouble?"

Mundro made a grimace. "Little annoyances just to let me know he could stomp me like a bug, whenever he felt like it. Some wire cut and a couple of steers shot. A water hole fouled and a fire set on the north side of the barn. Burned quite a hole there before I managed to get it out."

"Goddamn them," Rush said passionately. "Did Tabor know about it?"

"I told him. He couldn't do much. I didn't have any proof. He laid the law down to them. It's kinda tapered off."

His eyes were thoughtful. "You know, I had the feeling Ben wasn't as much behind it as Odie. I think those things came out of Odie's head. He works like hell to impress his

24

father. I feel sorta sorry for him. He's trying to fill Dan's boots, and he'll never make it."

"I don't feel sorry for him," Rush growled. "And he'd better stay off of here."

Mundro placed his hand on Rush's arm. "I think he will now that you're back. It's been a long time, son."

Rush felt the gentle pressure of his fingers. "Too long."

Both of them were skirting a subject that was bearing heavily on them, and Mundro took hold of it squarely.

"Do you want to see your mother's grave?"

"Yes." Rush's face was tight with strain. His memories of her were all good, and they made the aching, hollow loss harder to bear.

She was buried beside her parents near the great, scraggly tree. Rush remembered how she loved the shade of that old tree. On the other side of her was a smaller grave. Rush's brother was buried there. He hadn't lived to be two years old, and Rush hardly remembered him. Someday Mundro would be there with her, and maybe he welcomed it.

"She worried a lot about you being gone," Mundro said in a thin, flat voice. "She never believed you killed Dan. Not the way he was killed. She tried to hold on until you came back. And she never doubted that you would. I noticed she was looking bad, but she never complained. Then one morning I woke up, and she was gone. Doc Somers said she just wore out."

Rush cursed silently. This damned country wrung a person out until there was nothing left to them. Then it just threw them away.

His face went strained with anguish as he heard the harsh, wrenching sobs tearing Mundro apart. There wasn't a word he could say, or a gesture he could make. There wasn't a thing he could do to help Mundro Sawyer.

He walked to the far side of the tree and stared blindly into the distance. Mundro must have spent a lot of minutes doing that, and the knowledge increased Rush's agony.

He didn't know how long he stood there. He felt Mun-

25

dro's hand on his shoulder, and Mundro said, "Sorry, Rush. Sometimes it just gets to be more than I can bear."

"Sure," Rush said gruffly. He thought wildly, Mundro had no reason to apologize to him. He wished he could find the release Mundro found.

"Let's go get supper started," Mundro said, and his voice was almost normal. "Things are going to be better now that you're back."

Rush hoped Mundro was right. He was going to break his back to make it come out like Mundro said.

IV

THE WORRY started screwing its heavy pressure against Rush before the following morning was out. The winter kill had been higher than usual, and the spring rains had been scanty. As a result, the grass was late getting started. The cows were still winter gaunt, and those ribs and backbones would show until the grass strengthened.

"The damned varmints took a deep bite too," Mundro said. His tone was flat and unemotional, the tone of a man who had been hit so many times that he didn't even feel another blow. "Ever since the trappers pulled out, the wolves have poured in. We ran a few wolf drives, but we didn't kill a drop in the bucket."

Rush pulled up beside the remains of a cow and stared somberly at it. It was a good thing a rancher had a daily sleep period, a time to break the worry for at least a few hours, or otherwise, it would grind him to dust.

The uneven, pitiful struggle was written plainly in the earth. The winter-weakened cow had been unable to keep up with the herd, and some old dog wolf had marked her well. He had led the pack to her, and the scars in the ground, from her hooves as she whipped around to face first one of them, then the other, were sad to read. One of them had slipped in and hamstrung her, and her rear quarters had buckled and dumped her. She had slashed at the ground with her front hooves, still struggling to rise, until one of the pack had slipped in and torn out her throat. The pack had swarmed her then, and they didn't leave much of her. It meant one less calf for the spring crop, and the Sawyers could ill afford the loss.

Rush said savagely, "I'll fix them."

"How?" Mundro asked.

"Poison. Strychnine. I saw it used in Texas and Mexico."

Mundro looked dubious. "Isn't it dangerous?"

"Damned dangerous. Just smelling it can kill a man. I got just a whiff of it and thought I was going to die."

"Hell, Rush—" Mundro started. He saw the blaze in Rush's eyes and let the weak protest die.

"We'll get the ranchers together when we start to use it. It's deadly on dogs. They'll have to keep their hounds up."

Mundro shook his head. "They won't be happy about using stuff that dangerous."

"They'll be happier keeping the wolves?" Rush demanded.

Mundro sighed. "I guess not." He knew not. The ranchers would use anything if they could cut the wolves down.

"Maybe I can get it in Nyssa," Rush said. That was doubtful. He'd probably have to go to Ontario. He put a final look on the remains of the cow, and he was impatient to get started.

Yates was at the house when they returned. He drove a light spring wagon with bows, covered by a tarp. He said, "I'm going after supplies. Thought you might need something."

"I haven't been in for almost a month," Mundro said. "I've got a long list. I didn't have too much to feed Rush last night."

Rush grinned. They needed supplies, all right. Last night's supper had been on the skimpy side. "I'll ride in with you,

27

Jim." He squinted at the position of the sun. If he couldn't get strychnine in Nyssa, it would be too late to go on to Ontario. If a trip to Ontario was necessary, he could make it in the morning.

He saw the cloudbank in the northwest, a dark, sullen band lying just above the horizon.

"We going to get any rain out of that, Jim?"

"Maybe I jinxed it," Yates said. "I put the tarp on."

He was more than half serious. He had seen hundreds of those cloudbanks form and watched them with hope that finally faded just as the cloudbanks did.

Mundro went into the house and came back with his list. "Tell Crest to add it to our bill."

By the tightness around his mouth Rush suspected that the bill was old and big. A man worried about things like that.

He said, "Nope. I saved a little money and brought it back with me." It lacked a whole lot of being a fortune, but it would pay for a grocery bill.

He saw the tightness disappear. Mundro had known a struggle all right.

He climbed onto the seat beside Yates, and Mundro said, "Don't you get him drunk, Jim."

"Me get him drunk?" Yates said in mock astonishment. "It's always the other way around."

"I'll keep him in line, Mundro," Rush said and grinned.

He looked back after the wagon was in motion. Mundro raised his hand in a wave.

"He looks bad," he said.

"He looks a hundred percent better than he did," Yates answered. "You coming back lifted a big load off his shoulders."

Rush hoped so. He remembered the tight look about Mundro's mouth and asked, "Money's been scarce, hasn't it?"

"Money," Yates snorted. "What's that?" His face was gloomy. "Cattle prices are all shot to hell. If we're lucky and get the cows through the winter, the wolves take the calves. You see things going to pieces, and you can't do a

28

damned thing about it. What I couldn't do with a couple of thousand dollars." His swearing had a discouraged note. "I might as well ask for the moon. I've been seeing Leila for four years now. I can't ask her to marry me. What would I bring her home to?"

Rush knew what he meant. He could do a lot with a couple of thousand dollars, money that he could get in a lump sum —money that wasn't earmarked for bills run up between cattle shippings. It would make a lot of repairs; it would let a man catch up; it might even let him climb that last hill, that a man spent most of his life running on. He knew what Yates meant about Leila. He didn't have a girl, himself, but if he did have, he'd be in the same position. In this country, a man married pretty late. He had to because of sheer economic necessity.

"We might be able to do something about the wolves," he said.

He told Yates about the strychnine and saw the gleam appear in his eyes. "Mundro doesn't like it very well," he finished.

"Pa will feel the same way," Yates said. "But I'd try anything to get rid of them."

New ideas always met opposition. And sometimes the opposition could get pretty stubborn. But this was one time Rush wasn't going to let it get stubborn enough.

Yates ran his hand across the back of his neck. "I'm getting as shaggy as a damned sheep." He scowled into the distance, and Rush knew he was debating the price of a haircut against waiting another couple of weeks.

He said, "I need a haircut, myself. I'll treat you to a haircut and a bath." Yates put the frown on him, and Rush said quietly, "My coming-home present, Jim. Hell, you're getting so strong I can hardly sit next to you."

"Why, damn you," Yates exploded, then delight spread over his face. "A store-bought bath." It was a rarely-allowed luxury. "Maybe your coming back is changing things for the better."

Mundro had said something like that. Rush hoped both of them were right.

The bathhouse was behind the barber shop. Lucas Lamonte ran a clean place. He was a fussy man, with a pride in his establishment. He changed white coats every day and cleaned and polished the mirrors and windows until they sparkled. Rush couldn't remember ever seeing a fly-speck on them.

Lamonte was arguing with a man when Rush and Yates stepped into the shop. By the looks and smell of the man, Rush put him down as a sheepherder. His hair was wild and matted, and his beard was equally as tangled.

"You know my rules," Lamonte said heatedly. "You go out and buy new clothes before you take a bath in my place."

The man grumbled something, then turned and walked out of the door.

"Once a year they come in," Lamonte said indignantly. "Then I've got to cut away a year's growth and clean them up. I have to make them undress on newspapers to catch the lice. Then I have to burn their clothes."

"You may have insulted a customer, Lucas," Rush said and grinned.

Lamonte snorted. "Who cares? He'll probably pass a saloon and decide against spending his money for new clothes."

"Bring all the hot water you've got, Lucas," Yates ordered. "And don't bother me for a solid hour."

Rush did wait a half-hour before Yates was through. Yates was shining clean when he finally came into the barber shop.

"You took long enough," Rush said sourly.

"It took a long time to peel the layers of dirt off," Yates said solemnly. He climbed into a chair and ordered, "Cut me real close, Lucas. And put on plenty of your best stinkum. I may see Leila while I'm here." His eyes were half-closed in dreamy contemplation. "She don't often get a chance to see me all prettied up."

Rush luxuriated in the hot water and soap. When he came

out, Yates was inspecting himself in a mirror. His neck had a fresh, raw look.

He grinned at Rush's reflection in the mirror. "You want to smell me now? I didn't know I was so damned handsome."

"Lucas isn't that much of a magician," Rush said. "But he did make an improvement."

Yates started for the door, and Rush ordered, "Come back here. You're not leaving me until after we get the shopping done. I'm not waiting the rest of the afternoon and most of the night for you before we start."

Yates groaned, but he sat down and picked up a copy of a newspaper. "A month old," he said in disgust. "Lucas, don't you ever get anything new to read?"

It was old news, but Rush noticed he covered it thoroughly.

There was nothing like a hot towel and lather to send a man drifting. Lamonte chattered away, and Rush didn't hear half of what he said.

Lamonte finished, and Rush paid the bill. Yates inspected him critically. "He didn't make as much improvement in you as he did in me. But then he didn't have as much to work with." He ducked the punch Rush threw at him. "I owe you, Rush," he said gruffly.

"Sure," Rush agreed and followed him out of the shop.

"You go on into Crest's," Yates said. "I'll pull the wagon up in front." He peered up at the sky. "By God, I swear that cloudbank's moving."

Rush looked at it. The bank had thickened noticeably. A few hours ago, it covered only a thin segment of the horizon, now it stretched solidly as far as the eye coule see. It was an angry purplish black, and as he watched it, a jagged streak of lightning cut through it.

"Maybe we wasted the money for the baths," Yates said. "Maybe we should've waited for the rain." He whistled as he walked to the wagon. The hope was back stronger than ever, and maybe this time it wouldn't be denied.

Rush walked the block to Crest's store. Arnold Crest

31

was a thin, sunken-chested man, peering nearsightedly through rimless glasses. He was a sour man, seeing little to laugh at, but he was also patient. He carried families to the last step.

He said, "I heard you were back, Rush." He stuck out a limp hand. "I'm glad."

It wasn't an effusive greeting, but perhaps in his own way he meant it.

"I'm glad to be back," Rush answered. He pulled Mundro's list from his pocket. "I've got a long one today, Arnold."

A look of patient suffering appeared in Crest's eyes. He visualized this long list being added to the other credits.

"I want to pay for it," Rush said. "And catch up the old bill."

Crest brightened visibly, and there was a new spring in his step as he waited on Rush.

Yates came in during the middle of Rush's order. He looked at the growing pile of groceries on the counter and asked, "You planning on leaving anything for the next customer?"

Rush grinned. "Not much." He had slabs of bacon and paper bags of navy beans and big lima beans in that pile. Boxes of rice, oatmeal, and corn meal were heaped with sacks of flour and coffee. That was Arbuckle coffee, the best that Crest carried. Rush bought syrup and soda and baking powder, put up in paper boxes. He had dried prunes, dried apples, sugar and every other kind of staple he could think of. He ran through Mundro's skimpy list and kept ordering. For right now, at least, the Sawyer larder was going to be well stocked.

He finished and said, "Figure it up, Arnold, and add the old bill to it."

He sucked in his breath at the total. It sure as hell knocked a big hole in his savings. He looked at his few remaining dollars, then thrust them into his pocket. He wouldn't have Crest take back a thing on that long list.

"You'll eat for awhile," Yates commented and commenced his own ordering.

32

Rush waited until he was through, then said, "Arnold, I almost forgot the thing I wanted most. Have you got any strychnine?"

Crest's eyes grew round. "Strychnine? What in the world for?"

"He's thinking of poisoning me," Yates said solemnly. "But I'm too smart for him. I won't eat the damned stuff."

"Shut up, Jim," Rush said impatiently. "Wolf poison, Arnold." But he already had his answer. Crest didn't keep it in stock. "Anybody else in town handle it?"

Crest shook his head.

"Do you think I can get it in Ontario?"

"I'm not sure, Rush. Bethaney's might have it. He keeps a bigger stock than I do. Good Lord! Strychnine. That's the first call I've had for it since I've been in business."

Yates picked up an armload of groceries. "You might get another call for it in twenty or thirty years."

"Pick one of the heavy cans to throw at him," Rush advised.

He loaded up and followed Yates out of the store.

It took several trips to stow everything in the wagon. Yates dumped his last load and started down the street.

"Come back here," Rush ordered. "And help me secure this tarp. Look at that cloudbank."

Yates lifted his head skyward. The cloudbank was thick and ominous-looking, and a lighter line of gray clouds scudded along before it. Those running clouds denoted wind and lots of it. A jagged flash split the clouds, and distant thunder rumbled. A gust of wind blew down the street, stirring and lifting the dust and pushing it before it.

"Hot damn," Yates said. "Look at that. We're going to get a rain." His lips were smiling, but his eyes were sober. "I told you, you brought luck back with you."

"You're crazy," Rush jeered. This was the way a legend started. A man was on the scene when something happened, and it was attributed to him. If it happened again, the legend grew.

The wind was blowing in fitful gusts when the tarp was

33

finally tied down. Rush finished tying the rear flaps. He had debated trying to find shelter for the wagon, but there was none in town that he knew of. Hell, that tarp would turn the hardest downpour. As for the team, with all that dust in their hides, they would probably welcome rain.

"Come with me," Yates said impulsively. "Leila will be glad to see you."

It was a generous offer from a man who had too few hours with his girl.

Rush shook his head. "I've got some people I want to see. Will a couple of hours be enough?"

"I'll be back here by then," Yates promised.

He went down the walk with long, eager strides.

Rush felt a stab of wistfulness as he watched him. Something lonely and restless stirred within him, and he knew its source. Maybe he'd find somebody one of these days who would be glad to see him.

He started down the street, and Sam Tabor came around the corner. He said, "It looks like rain, Rush."

He had more than the weather on his mind, and Rush waited.

"Going to be in town long?" Tabor asked.

"You got a law against that?"

"Goddamnit, Rush," Tabor flared. He checked himself and said, "If you are, I'll tell you that Odie is in town. He's half-drunk and doing some mouthing. I thought you might want to keep an eye on him."

Rush's face softened. "Thanks, Sam."

Tabor gave him a bleak grin and moved on.

Rush stood for a moment in indecision. He had intended buying a drink or two, but now he decided against it. He had no fear of Odie, but there was no sense in looking for trouble, either. And it wouldn't be hard to find in a half-drunk, quarrelsome man.

He cut across the street toward Brad Wilkie's saddle shop. A man could while away some pleasant time in there.

Just before he stepped inside the clap of thunder sounded

34

so near it made him start. The wind blew steadily down the street, carrying the cooling effect of nearby rain.

Wilkie looked up from the saddle he was working on, and smiled his greeting. He said, "Rush, it's good to see you." He made no attempt to rise, and Rush suspected his rheumatism had gotten worse. Brad had been pretty crippled before he left.

He took the bent and crippled hand, the hand that still had so much skill in it when it came to carving leather, and grinned his pleasure.

Wilkie was a little, stooped man, with skin as tough and colored as the leather he worked on. He must have been pushing eighty, but his eyes were as bright and clear as ever.

Wilkie snorted. "I told Sam Tabor he had the wrong man locked up. But with Ben Cavanaugh hollering at him, I guess he couldn't go any other way."

"Ben's still blaming me."

"The goddamned old fool. He can't reach Clayton. He can reach you. And he's got to have somebody to take his mean out on."

"You don't sound very fond of him."

Wilkie snorted again. "He's got more money than anybody around here. And he's still the slowest pay. He owes me for a saddle I made for him a couple of years ago. I'll never do another job for him until he pays me cash in advance."

The shop was filled with the sweet smell of saddle leather. The room was hung with straps of the material, and benches and tables were piled high with it. Knives were all over the place, and Rush knew better than to test any of their edges. Wilkie kept sharp knives.

He and Wilkie were the only ones here now, but it was a favorite hanging-out place for cowmen. The spittoon before the store showed much use, and the floor around it was stained with poorly aimed shots.

Wilkie built a tough saddle, but he didn't neglect beauty. The one he was working on had hand-carved roses that took a horseman's eye. All of the parts were made by hand. It

35

took a craftsman to build the swell, the seat, and the horn into a comfortable-fitting saddle. Then the skirt rig, the stirrups, and cinch had to be assembled with equal care. Wilkie wasn't satisfied with just building a practical saddle. His hand carving and embossing was a work of art.

"Aren't you about ready for a new saddle?" Wilkie asked.

"I sure am," Rush said fervently. His old saddle was pretty scratched and battered. But the saying of it was about as far as he could go now.

He heard the first hard drops slash against the window and moved to it. The drops were making quarter-sized pocks in the dusty street.

"We're going to get a good one, Brad," he said jubilantly.

Wilkie stood and hobbled to him. The rain was enough for a crippled man to make the effort to see it.

"It's about time," Wilkie said.

Somebody jerked the bottom out of the clouds, and the rain came down in buckets.

They stood for a half-hour, watching the rain. It was still raining hard when they sat down again, but Rush didn't think it would last long. Usually, a hard storm petered out in fairly short order. But it would do a lot of good. Already, the street was running rivulets.

He spend a pleasant two hours talking to Wilkie before the rain stopped. He stood and looked out the window. "About over," he said. He would wade mud to reach the wagon.

"Come back," Wilkie called as Rush went out of the door.

"I will," Rush said.

The mud squished around his boots as he stepped off the walk. It would take double the time going back home. But he wasn't objecting at all.

The rain had stopped, but the clouds were slow in drifting away. They would make for an early evening. He was halfway across the street, when he saw something unusual about the wagon. He had to think about it to catch it. The bows were naked. The tarp had been stripped off of them.

Anger and dismay raced through him as he reached the wagon. The tarp lay beside it, beaten into the mud by the rain. He had never seen such a goddamned mess in the bed.

The beans were soaked and swollen, and the prunes and dried apples were the same way. They were bulging out through their paper boxes and mingling with the broken, soggy bean sacks. The soda and baking-powder boxes had broken open, and their contents were fizzing. The rice, flour, and oatmeal were turning to a doughy mass, and the stopper was out of the jug of syrup. The two bags of Arbuckle coffee were right in the middle, and everything was ruined.

He was swearing helplessly, when Yates came up.

Yates thought his swearing was directed at him, and he said, "I'm not more than fifteen minutes late."

"Look at it," Rush said in a rage-choked voice. "Somebody cut the tarp strings and stripped it off."

Yates looked at the mess, and his swearing was more vicious than Rush's. He ran down and asked, "Who?"

"Tabor told me Odie was in town."

"Why, that son-of-a-bitch," Yates said. "Let's find him."

Rush spotted Tabor coming up the street. "Wait a minute. I want him to see this. Sam," he called. "Come here."

Tabor's mouth sagged as he looked at the ruined groceries.

"Who?" he finally managed to ask.

"You know who," Rush snapped. "Odie Cavanaugh. You saw that tarp on the bows. Somebody stripped it off. Who else would do it but Odie."

Tabor saw the fury in Rush's eyes. "You've got to get proof, Rush. Don't go jumping him without it. Bring me proof, and I'll see he pays for everything."

"Let's go find him," Yates said grimly.

"I'm going with you," Tabor said. His face grew angry. "Damnit. I'm trying to keep you out of trouble."

Odie wasn't in town. They looked all over for him. And they couldn't find anybody who had seen Oddie near the wagon.

"Who pays for it now?" Yates howled.

"We do," Rush said wearily. He could see Tabor's side.

37

Maybe Tabor knew it was Odie's work, too, but he couldn't let them do anything about it without proof.

"I'm going to kill that son-of-a-bitch one of these days," Yates said.

"You'll stand in line," Rush replied.

"Stop that kind of talk," Tabor said sharply. "Rush, I'm sorry."

Defeat was in Rush's face. "Oh, go to hell."

He turned and plodded back to the wagon, and Yates followed him.

They borrowed a shovel from Crest and scooped out the mess. Rush's second buying wasn't nearly as elaborate as his first. And he had to put it on the books. The Sawyers were back in debt again.

Yates' shoulders drooped as he climbed to the seat and picked up the reins. "Rush, it's my fault. If I hadn't stopped to see Leila—"

"Stop it," Rush said savagely. "We both know who's fault it is." He stared bleakly ahead. *All right, Odie,* he thought. *It's your turn now.* Odie must have howled with delight all the way home. He'd better howl good, while he could.

He said. "Jim, don't say anything to Mundro about this." Mundro had enough burdens to carry, without adding to them.

V

RUSH RODE TO Ontario the following day. The rain had done some good. He swore he could see the grass thrusting upwards under the stimulus of it. This was a day to delight a cattleman's heart, if it hadn't been for the ruined groceries. He had cursed Odie Cavanaugh a thousand times, and he still couldn't wash it from his mind. If Odie so much as cut his eyes at him the next time they met, Rush intended beating his head off.

Ontario was a much bigger town than Nyssa. It lay some twelve miles up the Snake River, but by cutting the diagonal from home Rush had lessened the distance.

It had been quite a few years since he had been here, and he was interested in the town's growth. The first building of the business district, had a sign that read, *Julia's Laundry*, and the size of the building surprised him. It was made of logs, and he guessed it to be twenty feet wide and thirty feet long. It must be a successful business to need that much space.

The slender figure toiling at the side of the building caught his interest. The person was dressed in jeans and a man's rough work shirt. He had his back toward him and, at first, Rush thought it was a boy, struggling with a job too heavy for him. He was apparently trying to cover a ditch that led from the side of the building to the river, and some of the poles he was using were too heavy.

The boy bent over to lift another pole, and Rush's eyes widened. That was no boy. There was too much rounded fullness in the rear of those jeans.

He swung down and said, "Let me give you a hand."

The woman straightened and turned. Her face was flushed from her exertions, and Rush thought some flicker of recognition filled her eyes. But he must be mistaken. To the best of his knowledge he had never seen her before.

He judged her to be about twenty, and she had all of a woman's enticing roundness. He wouldn't say she was beautiful, but her face commanded attention. The eyes were magnificent, a deep blue with a rare purity of color. Her broad face was strong and resourceful, with high, prominent cheekbones. The nose was too large, the mouth too wide and mobile for genuine beauty, but he had never known a generous-mouthed woman to be shrewish of nature. She had a level way of looking at a man that probed deep, and he'd hate to try to lie to her.

39

She said, "This one is almost too much for me," and tapped the offending log with the toe of her boot.

He upended and dragged it to the ditch. He laid it beside all the others and saw what she was trying to do. She was covering the ditch with the poles, then shoveling dirt over them. But he wondered why.

She answered the question in his eyes. "We empty our tubs into the ditch, and it drains into the river. But the townspeople complained about the ditch smelling, and four people have fallen into it." Her eyes twinkled. "All of them were drunk. But one of them was the mayor."

Rush said solemnly, "And that made the difference."

"The big difference." Her free and easy laughter rang out.

He joined in the laughter, and it was a rich, shared moment. "We wouldn't want that happening to His Honor again. I'll give you a hand."

He didn't wait for her consent. He picked up the poles and laid them in the ever-extending row. She had twenty feet of the ditch covered, but she still had quite a way to go to the river. It took a lot of work at the moment, but if she could continue to use the ditch, it would more than make up for it later. Dumping the soiled water at the building would save many a step to the river. He wondered how she ever managed to carry a tub of water that far.

She followed behind him, shoveling dirt onto the poles until it was mounded up. She fell far behind, for her work took more time.

He worked an hour without stopping, and he wished he had enough time to stay and finish the job.

She said, "That's enough. I had no hope I'd get a fifth this far all day." She leaned on the shovel, and her bosom rose and fell from her exertions. It was hard for him to keep from watching the fascinating movement.

He said gravely, "His Honor can't fall into this part of it now. But he might trip over it."

The sound of her laughter was a delight. Here was a woman who would fill a house with it.

She insisted upon him coming in for a cup of coffee.

40

"It's already made." She wrinkled her nose. "It's poor pay for what you've done."

"Ample pay," he said. Just being around her was pay enough.

Inside the building, tubs sat on long benches. He looked around with a lively curiosity, and she warmed to it.

She said, "We started the business eighteen months ago." She grimaced at some rough memory. "It was slow going at first. But things picked up enough to keep us encouraged. We do the laundry with elbow grease and washboards. I wonder how may buckets of water I've carried from the river." She looked at her hands with mock dismay. "And what it's doing to my hands." She shook her head in disparagement, but it was plain to see that she was proud of her accomplishments. "We turn out a nice job of ironing." She pointed to the heavy irons with their attached handles, heating on the wood-burning cookstove. "How much wood I've fed that hungry monster."

Rush knew it took a lot of wood to heat the water necessary and the irons. Those irons cooled off pretty fast, even though at first one had to pad the handle to be able to hold it.

"The cowboys are our best customers," she said. She pointed to the pegs driven along the walls, with a man's name over each peg. "After their clothes are washed and ironed, they're hung on the pegs under their names. Some of the townswomen are even beginning to come to us."

She said "We" and "Our" and "Us," but at the moment she was the only one here. She poured him a cup of coffee, and he shook his head at the offer of cream and sugar.

He sipped at it and said, "If your laundry is as good as your coffee, I'd be a steady customer."

She smiled her thanks, and a faint tinge of color crept up from the collar of her shirt.

He refused a second cup, and the regret in his voice was real as he said, "I've got to be getting on."

She walked with him to the door. "I'm grateful to you."

"For nothing," he said brusquely. He looked back after a

half-dozen strides. She was still there, and she was smiling at him.

Bethaney's was twice as big a store as Crest's. Rush asked for his strychnine, and the clerk said, "We've got some somewhere. Not many calls for it."

He turned and walked into a rear room. He was gone fifteen minutes before he returned with a dust-covered box. "Let me wrap it," he said. "This stuff is dangerous, you know."

Rush nodded. "I've handled it before."

He said casually as the clerk wrapped the package, "That's quite a laundry you've got in town."

"Julia's done all right," the clerk answered, and that was pride in his voice. "She opened it, after her mother died. She hired three dance hall girls, who were getting too old to compete with the fresher ones." That was a touch of malice in his grin. "The women of the town squawked their heads off at first about her running a business with those kind of women. The squawking's dying now. Julia does good work. Do you know Julia and those other three built that building almost by themselves. They got a little help now and then, but that doesn't take any credit away from them."

"It sure doesn't," Rush said and walked outside.

He stowed the strychnine in a saddlebag and mounted. This Julia sounded like quite a girl. He had more than suspected it when he saw her fighting that ditch. He wondered if he had properly thanked her for the coffee and grinned. Anyway, it was an excuse to stop back by for a moment.

He swung down and tied his reins to the rack before the laundry. He heard an angry voice and the sound of scuffling coming from the building. He stepped in on quite a scene.

A burly man had his arms wrapped around Julia, and her face was a furious mask as she tried to free herself.

Rush heard her say, "Hige, if you don't let go of me and get out of here—"

Another woman clawed at one of Hige's arms, trying to pull it free. He swept it back suddenly, catching her across the mouth with the forearm. The impact smashed her back into a wall, and she slid down it, her face dazed. The twin

42

impacts must have really scattered her senses, for she sat at the base of the wall making no attempt to get up.

Hige said, "You've put me off long enough, Julia."

Rush took four long strides and clamped a hand on Hige's shoulder. He jerked him backwards and spun him around. His voice was almost pleasant. "Didn't you hear what the lady said? Or are you too thickheaded to understand?"

He had a glimpse of that face changing from startled surprise to fury. It was a heavy-boned face, and the features were cut thick. The eyes were small, and that meanness looked natural in them.

Rush planted his fist in the middle of that big-lipped mouth. It was an effective stopper against the invective that was beginning to pour out of it.

He had a lot of anger riding on the punch, and it doubled its force. It knocked Hige out of the side door, and he stumbled over the mounded-up dirt of the ditch. Hige was pretty drunk: it showed in his uncoordinated movements, in his slow recovery time. But even drunk he could absorb the lesson Rush intended giving him.

He charged Hige and hit him again, driving him along the course of the ditch. Somebody on the street yelled, and he heard the sound of running feet. Nothing drew an audience quicker than a fight.

Hige's hands were pawing, and his feet were unsteady when Rush hit him the third time. It drove Hige past the last of the mounded-up dirt, past the poles Rush had laid. He had Hige where he wanted him, and the open, soap-scummed, muddy ditch lay behind him.

Hige's mouth was open and gasping for air when Rush hit him again. Rush felt a sharp stab of pain in the knuckles of his right hand and thought mournfully that he was giving that hand a lot of punishment these last few days.

The blow knocked Hige backwards, and he fell into the ditch. He rolled over and tried to get to his feet. He made it halfway and hung there a moment. The dozen men who had gathered broke into howls of laughter. Hige was filthy with slimy mud. His foot slipped, and he went down again.

Julia stood in the side door, and her face was white.

Rush put a last look on Hige. The man was threshing about in the ditch, trying to regain his footing. Rush doubted that any more fight was on his mind.

He approached Julia, and she said, "He won't forget that."

Rush grinned. Hige wouldn't. At least, as long as that mud clung to him. He said, "I'll worry about it later."

She cried "You're hurt. You're bleeding."

He looked at his hand, and blood was dripping from it. He started to raise it to suck on it, and she commanded, "Don't do that. Come inside and let me take care of it."

She cleansed the wound, and he said, "I must've cut it on Hige's teeth." He wouldn't be sorry to hear he had broken a couple of them.

"This will sting," she said. She poured liquid from a bottle on it, and she put her estimate too low. He wanted to swear against the burning.

The woman Hige had knocked down hovered around them, and Julia said, "This is Lily Burns."

"Did he hurt you?" Rush asked.

Lily shook her head. She was somewhere in her high thirties, and hard experiences had made harsh inroads upon her face.

"I'd like to kill him," she said viciously. "He's always bothering Julia. He's killer mean. He's gunned down three men that I know of. Everybody in town's afraid of him."

Rush shrugged.

"Don't take him lightly," Lily warned. "Hige Mercer won't forget this."

"Let him worry about it," Rush said.

He blew on his knuckles again. The stinging was easing off.

Julia walked with him to the hitchrack. The crowd had gone, and Hige Mercer was nowhere in sight.

"Lily's right," she said, and her eyes were concerned. "Hige will be looking for you."

"I won't duck him."

"I'm grateful for everything you did for me," she said in a low voice.

He wondered if she felt as he did—reluctant to end this moment. He said hopefully, "Maybe I'll be riding to Ontario again soon."

Color was in her face, but she met his eyes steadily, "I hope so," and more than just politeness was in her tone.

VI

TABOR'S EYES were concerned as he listened. "Did you warn everybody to keep their dogs up?"

"I've been riding for a solid week," Yates complained. "Hell, we told people in Wyoming, Montana, and Nebraska we were putting out poison."

Rush gave him an unfeeling grin. They had covered the country pretty good. Now and then they had run into a little opposition. It was just natural for a man to hate having poison lying around.

"We didn't warn the Cavanaugh's," he said.

"Why not?" Tabor exploded. "You know how proud Ben is of his bear hounds. If you're trying to get back at Ben—"

Rush sighed patiently. "We kept off their land to keep from riling them."

"Rush, did you ever notice how some men pop off without using their heads?" Yates asked caustically.

"We waited until the Cavanaughs were in town," Rush said. "They'll take the warning more seriously coming from you, Sam."

Tabor colored. Why didn't Rush tell him that first instead of letting him make a fool of himself? The damned, young smart-alecs. They'd nicely baited a trap for him, and he had stepped into it.

"Where are they?" he growled.

"They were in Wakeman's," Yates said solemnly. "Rush, don't it do your heart good to see a lawman afoaming and faunching to be off at his duty?"

"It sure does," Rush said with equal gravity.

Tabor swore at them. The glint was brighter in their eyes. "You two are going to be with me when I tell them."

The glint disappeared from Rush's eyes. "Sam, do you think that's wise? Just the sight of us—"

"I know just how they feel," Tabor said with malice. "I'll make the warning official. You can tell them just what can happen. Not that they'll listen to either of us."

They walked into Wakeman's, and Odie Cavanaugh's face tightened. "He can't prove a damned thing," he said. "It's his word against mine."

Ben swore at him, and Odie fell sullenly silent.

"What am I trying to prove, Odie?" Rush asked. Those ruined groceries were on Odie's mind. It was as plain as though he had shouted it.

"Stop it," Tabor said. "Ben, I want you to listen good. The ranchers have gotten together and are putting out wolf poison tomorrow. Keep your hounds up for several days."

Ben's eyes swung from Tabor to Rush. "His idea?"

"What difference does it make?" Yates said hotly. "You want those wolves killed, don't you?"

"You're not coming on my land," Ben shouted.

Rush checked Yates' outburst. A man had to keep a tight rein on his temper around these two. There was just no talking to them.

"We didn't have any intention of stepping on your land," he said evenly. "But we can't keep the wolves off it. A wolf will head for the nearest water after he's been poisoned. If he dies on your land and one of your hounds finds him, he's a dead dog."

"Are you going to let him put out something that dangerous?" Ben demanded.

"You'd argue with Jesus Christ, wouldn't you?" Tabor asked

46

in disgust. "If you lose some hounds, don't come screaming to me about it."

He turned on his heel, and Rush and Yates followed him. Ben's shouting followed them onto the street.

Yates grinned. "He's a hardheaded old bastard."

"He's going to lose his hounds, Sam." Rush's eyes were concerned. "I've seen it happen."

"You've done everything you can," Tabor said testily. He could see trouble coming from this. What was he fretting about? One way or another—didn't it always come?

"Do me a favor, will you?" he asked. "Don't take any particular pains to cut their path."

He expected objections, at least from Yates. But Yates only sighed and said. "That rules out Wakeman's. And it was our favorite drinking place."

They went off down the street together, and their laughter drifted back to Tabor. Tabor watched them go and envied them their companionship.

He sighed and turned to make a round of the town. A lawman never knew any real peace. Even when it was quiet, he worried about the unnaturalness of it.

He passed Wakeman's coming back to his office and upon sudden impulse stepped into it. Without the sight of Rush goading Ben Cavanaugh maybe he could talk some sense into his head.

He stopped inside the door. He recognized the hulk that was draped over the bar. Hige Mercer was in earnest conversation with the Cavanaughs. Tabor knew the swath Mercer had cut in Ontario. He was a bully with a hair-trigger temper and some skill with a gun. It was inevitable that some day somebody would put a bullet into him. But that day wasn't here yet. He cast about for some reason to throw Mercer in jail or run him out of town. So far, Mercer hadn't broken any law he knew of. Legally, he couldn't touch him. He backed out of the door. None of the three had noticed him. All he could do was to keep an eye on Mercer. He shook his head. Mercer and the Cavanaughs with their heads together. That was a sticky mess for somebody. He

47

swore in sudden anger. Hadn't he predicted trouble was coming?

"We'd better be getting back, Jim," Rush said. He knew that bright shine in Yates' eyes. A few more drinks, and nobody could pry Yates away from this bar.

He saw the argument in Yates' eyes and snapped, "All right. I'll get somebody else to help me in the morning."

The belligerence faded in Yates' face. "Aw, Rush, you wouldn't do that to me."

"You think I want some hung-over bum backing me up in the morning? I'm scared enough as it is to handle the stuff."

That was the right appeal, for Yates said, "What are we standing around here for?"

Rush nodded and hid his grin. He'd dangled the right bait in front of Yates.

They'd taken a half-dozen steps toward the door when a voice bawled, "Sawyer, I know you're in there. Do I have to come in and drag you out?"

"That didn't sound like any friendly voice, Rush." The words were light, but the look in Yates' eyes wasn't. "Who is it?"

Rush wasn't certain. He had heard Mercer's voice for such a brief time. But it sounded like him.

"Let me go out and look around," Yates said.

"He didn't ask for you, Jim."

"I was afraid you'd remember that," Yates said.

Rush pushed through the door, and Mercer was planted on wide-spread legs in the middle of the street. His eyes were cold sober and mean-looking. He said in mock surprise, "I sure thought I'd have to drag you out."

Rush eyed him levelly. Mercer was big, and he should have stuck to his fists for he was no gunman. He wore his holster too high, and his hand dangled far below the butt. He would have to cock and throw that elbow high before he could clasp the butt, and that would take the vital split second that made the difference.

48

"Mercer," Rush said slowly. "I got no quarrel with you."

Yates was behind and to one side of him, and Rush could hear the careful rasp of his breathing.

"That sure makes us different," Mercer said. "Because I got one with you. You've got a poor choice. If you face me, I'll puncture your gut. If you try to run, I'll shoot your ass off."

Mercer's little success with a gun had gone to his head. He was bound to step out of his class, and somebody would drop him. Rush just wished it didn't have to be him. Something the old Texan had said popped into his mind. "If you ever point a gun at a man, don't get cute and try to wing him. He could still get off a shot that could finish you. If you've got enough reason to point a gun at him, you've got enough reason to kill him."

A block down the street a voice shouted sounding thin and distorted with its anger. "Hold it," Tabor yelled.

Tabor was going to be too late to break this up. Mercer's face said he wasn't going to let anybody stop this.

Rush kept his eyes fastened on Mercer's face and right shoulder. When a decision was reached, something would flicker in those eyes, and the muscles in shoulder and arm would jump. He stood there easy and relaxed-looking and said almost pleasantly, "All right, big mouth. You pushed this."

Mercer's face contorted. His shoulder dipped, and he started his grab for the gun. He wasn't good, and the men he had killed must have been remarkably bad. A smooth draw was as fluid as flowing water, and Mercer didn't have it.

Rush waited until Mercer's hand touched the gun butt before he drew. He slammed the bullet into the peak of the arch of the rib cage, and it carried tremendous shocking force. It lifted Mercer high on his toes, and he still struggled to get his gun out. He clawed it free, but the strength was fading too fast from his arm to lift it. He looked at Rush with dazed, disbelieving eyes. He seemed to stretch even higher, and without volition a constricting finger pulled the

49

trigger. The bullet dug into the street near his right foot. He started bending at the middle then broke all at once and pitched on his face.

This was the second time Rush had known this sickness. At first, he thought his stomach would empty, and the sourness of that sickness rose into his throat.

It seemed an eternity before the sickness was under control. He realized he still stared at Mercer, at the bleeding that pushed red fingers out into the street, and he jerked his eyes from him.

Men were beginning to move out from the doorways of buildings, and the awe in their eyes was still big enough to hold them speechless.

Tabor stopped beside Rush, and he panted hard. Some kind of defeat was in his face as he said, "You had to have it this way."

Yates bounded out beside Rush, and his face was all belligerence. "He didn't want it this way. He was called out. What did you expect him to do?"

Rush waved him quiet. In a vague way he understood the defeat in Tabor's face.

"He wouldn't budge, Sam. I ran into him in Ontario. He was manhandling a woman. I knocked him into a muddy ditch, and people laughed at him. I guess he couldn't forget it."

"He's forgotten it now," Tabor said sourly.

"If you're blaming Rush—" Yates started hotly.

"Shut up," Tabor yelled. His face was red with anger, anger directed at himself. He should have done something when he first saw Mercer. He knew that now.

"I saw it," he said and glared at Yates.

"Will you want me, Sam?" Rush asked.

"I'll want a report. Go to my office and wait for me."

"You putting him under arrest?" Yates asked incredulously.

Before Tabor could explode, Rush said, "Keep still, will you, Jim?"

He turned and walked down the street and, after a moment's indecision, Yates followed him.

Tabor hurried toward Wakeman's. If the Cavanaughs were still in town, he had to get them out. He knew the burden a killing put on a man. It stretched his nerves fine and muddied his thinking. If Rush learned the Cavanaughs had a hand in this, there was no telling how he'd react.

He found them standing in front of the saloon, their faces drawn tight from some kind of waiting.

Odie's eagerness showed. "Did I hear a couple of shots? I thought maybe there was a—"

"A fight?" Tabor finished for him. "There was. A man got himself killed. He tried to draw against a better man."

Odie's face began crinkling into little lines of pleasure.

"You sonuvabitch," Tabor raged. "I saw you talking to him. You told him where he could find Rush, didn't you?"

Odie blinked, and his jaw sagged. He recovered quickly, but he'd marked himself. "You can't blame me," he squalled. "I wasn't even near that fight."

Ben Cavanaugh tasted something sweet. "A man killed," he said. "Now, isn't that awful."

Tabor took their happy moment away from him. "Rush shot him before he could clear his gun. Keep on plaguing Rush, Odie, and the same thing's going to happen to you. Keep on giving him reasons, and I won't lift a finger to stop it."

Their faces turned a doughy gray. Right now, they had hollows instead of stomachs, and Tabor enjoyed seeing it. If they didn't get a picture from what had happened, they were too damned stupid to live. *And they won't,* Tabor thought grimly as he turned and moved away.

VII

Twenty ranchers and hands gathered at the Sawyer ranch in the morning. They knew about the gun fight, it was in their eyes, but none of them asked questions about it. Tabor

51

was here, and at first, Rush thought it was official business. But curiosity had pulled him the same as it had pulled the others.

Rush had the package he had brought back from Ontario and several big hunks of tallow laid out before him. He had lectured Yates long and earnestly last night about the danger of this stuff, and he thought Yates was impressed.

"Stand back all of you," he said. "Just a whiff of this stuff can make you damned sick. I saw a man almost die that way."

He waited until they moved back a respectful distance, then pulled his neckerchief up around his nose and mouth. He pulled on light leather gloves, and Yates did the same.

"Hell," some wit called. "They're not fixing to poison wolves. They're ready to rob the bank."

Most of them laughed, and it pulled a pained grin from Tabor. Some of the old-timers watched with frowning eyes. Mundro was one of them. They didn't like any part of this idea.

Rush broke off a chunk of tallow as big as his balled fist. Even in the sunlight the stuff was hard and unworkable. He beat it with a rock until it softened. Once it was broken down he could mold it with his hands. He cut a twig six inches long and whittled on it until it was flattened on one end. Then he poked a hole in the ball of tallow and started dribbling the deadly crystals into it.

"It won't work," somebody said from behind him. "Wolves are too smart to take aholt of something humans touch."

Rush pinched the hole shut. "Meat carries human scent," he said. "Tallow won't." His voice sounded muffled because of the mask. "Jim, make me some more balls."

He had a plentiful supply of tallow on hand. He had asked every cowman to bring in a chunk of it.

His audience stirred restlessly as the slow process of building and poisoning the tallow balls went on. One of them asked, "You going to make a million of them?"

Rush looked at the gunny bag. It was better than half filled.

"I guess that'll do," he said. Three cow carcasses had been reported to him, and he had the sites marked in his head. By the time he poisoned them and the beef stomachs he would be out of strychnine.

He straightened and rolled his shoulders, easing the ache in them. He had been bent over for a long time.

He handed Yates a couple of gunny bags to carry. Those stomaches were messy even inside of a bag. They were beginning to leak through.

Yates stowed the bags on his restless horse and grumbled at it, "You won't be any happier than I will when this is over."

He started to pull down his neckerchief, and Rush warned, "Leave it alone. You might've gotten some of it on your gloves."

He looked at Tabor and said, "Sam, I want you to ride with us. I want you to see every place we bait."

Tabor nodded and moved to his horse. The rest started to follow, and Rush ordered them back. "It'll hurt us if all of us go crashing through the brush wiping scent all over it. If a wolf catches it, he won't come near the bait. And he'd do almost anything to get a piece of tallow."

He looked at all the glum faces. They didn't believe in this very much. All he could tell them was it had worked in Mexico.

He found the first carcass and kept Tabor and Yates well away from it. He sprinkled poison into the sad remains of the cow. He made sure the wind was in the right direction, and kept his head turned as much as he could while he worked.

He finished and joined Yates and Tabor. "We'll have to come out in a few days and burn what's left of that carcass. The bones can pick up the poison. And you know how cattle like to mouth old bones?"

Yates nodded, and Tabor asked curiously, "What makes you think the wolves will come back here, Rush?"

"A wolf won't make a fresh kill until he finishes up the old one. A carcass can't get too rank to keep him away."

53

He mounted and appeared to be riding aimlessly. But he was looking for a wolf run. A wolf was as single-minded as a cow critter. They'd follow the old trails rather than make new ones. He looked where the terrain was the easiest. A wolf didn't like any more difficulties with his going than a man did.

He found the first trail weaving between two hills. He studied it and said, "They've been along here not too long ago."

He picked a single brushy plant, near the run, and said, "Watch me, Jim. Don't let your horse, your chaps, or your tapaderos touch any part of the brush. It'll leave a scent a wolf can pick up."

He rode up to the bush, picked the least brushy side, and leaned over. He siezed the tip of a branch about four feet off the ground and slashed it off with his other hand. It left an angled, sharp-pointed spike. He impaled a tallow ball on it and carried the cut-off part a long way before he dropped it.

Yates nodded. "I see. You carried off the only part you touched."

"That's it," Rush said.

They baited that trail and found another. It was slow, tedious work because of the care a man must exercise.

Yates impaled the last tallow ball and started to drop the empty gunny bag. He caught Rush's eyes on him and colored. "You act like they're smarter than we are."

"Sometimes, I think they are," Rush said soberly.

He poisoned the two remaining carcasses and he had about four tablespoons of Strychrine left. That was just about right for the stomachs.

He opened the first gunny bag and gagged at the smell. It made a man's stomach turn over to drag out that mess. He had stuffed the entrails, the heart, and the clotted blood into the stomachs, and he divided the poison between the two.

He hung them up about five feet high from a branch that

54

stretched over a run and poked tiny holes into them. The reeking mess started a slow, slimy drip.

"That's pretty high, isn't it?" Tabor asked.

"I've seen where wolves passed it up because it was too easy," Rush answered. "They apparently like to work for it. If they get to fighting over it, it makes them more determined than ever."

The sun was getting low. The baiting had taken most of the day.

Rush reached back after he had ridden a long way and jerked the knot in the neckerchief loose. He let it drop to the ground. He stripped off his gloves and stuffed them into his saddlebag.

Yates did the same. "I've been suffocating all day," he complained. "When do we start seeing dead wolves?"

Tabor waited with the same bright curiosity, and Rush said, "In a couple of days." Under his breath he added, *I hope.*

The ranchers were still waiting when they returned home. Rush had the same message for them, and it made them unhappy. Their impatience galled him, and he said, "Damnit, did you expect me to come in toting them? They've got to find the bait and eat it. Then the poison's got to have time to work. Look around the water holes the day after tomorrow, then come to me with that damned judging look."

He hoped he was right. He'd gone to a lot of preparation and built up hopes. A man didn't like to make himself look like a fool before everybody.

Tabor said before he rode off, "Hope it works, Rush."

Rush said in mean humor, "You just remember that none of that poison was put near the Cavanaughs."

He rode to a waterhole the next morning and was sick with disappointment when he saw no dead wolves. Strychnine built a raging thirst in a poisoned animal, and if possible he always made it to the nearest water.

Don't be a damned fool, he advised himself. *It's too early. You told them it'd be tomorrow.* Just the same he had had high hopes of seeing at least one dead wolf.

Yates rode over in the morning before Rush finished breakfast. His eyes were silver-dollar round and shining with excitement.

"You been out looking yet?"

"Not yet," Rush lied. "I thought I might go out pretty soon."

Yates was so eager to talk that he babbled. "You know that seep over in our northwest corner. They're three dead lobos stretched by it. Just as pretty as you please."

Rush let out a carefully held breath. This was what he had hoped for. This was fine, fine.

"Big devils," Yates said. "They were dead, but damned if I didn't want to pump bullets into them."

That wasn't hard to understand. A man looked at those wolves and remembered mangled cow flesh. He remembered calves that would never grow up and others that would never be born.

"You think there's more?" Yates asked.

"I wouldn't be surprised," Rush said gravely.

"Then let's go look," Yates yelled. He tugged on Rush's arm. If Rush wanted to finish his breakfast, he'd eat it in the saddle.

They met Colie Sanders before they'd ridden five miles, and Sanders had his two riders with him. All of them had broad, pleased grins.

Sanders hooked a knee over his saddle horn and rolled a cigarette. "What's new, Rush?"

Yates glared at him. "Damn you, Colie. What's tickling you so much this morning?"

"Do I look tickled?" Sanders asked innocently. "I can't imagine why. Do you, boys?"

His two riders shook their heads, and their grins spread.

"I'm going whip you," Yates howled. "I found three dead wolves this morning. How many did you find?"

Sanders could hold it no longer. "Five," he blurted. "Around my big water hole. How many of them do you think we got, Rush?"

Rush shook his head. He had no way of knowing. But

the number was mounting up nicely. There would be other riders out scouring the country. If they had the same kind of success to report, a big dent had been made in the wolf population.

"What are we sitting around here for?" Yates yelled and spurred off.

Every water hole, every seep of moisture pushed the toll higher. Rush looked at the dead animals and knew a hard satisfaction. He wondered how much beef that big, old wolf dog over there had pulled down. The animal was about as big a wolf as he had ever looked at. He guessed it to be nine feet from tip of nose to top of tail, and it should weigh about a hundred and fifty pounds. Its lips were drawn back in final agony, and even in death its fangs looked menacing.

"Big bastard, wasn't he?" Yates said and shook his head. "You know I'm enjoying this. I'd ride my ass off to count dead wolves."

They grinned at Yates, and their eyes were shining. They knew how he felt.

"Let's go see what happened to the stomachs I hung up," Rush said.

The stomachs were still hanging from their branches, but they were ragged and torn. The marks on the ground beneath them were plain to read. Eight or ten wolves had fought over the reeking contents of the stomachs.

"It looks like they fought each other pretty hard," Rush said. "The really good part of this is that for every dead one you find, maybe a couple didn't make it to water. They die out in the brush, and you never see them."

"No," Sanders said. He whooped with sudden delight. "That's the worst news I ever heard." He threw his hat in the air, spun his horse and dashed toward the hat. He leaned out of the saddle and swooped it up.

"Let's go find some more wolves," he yelled.

Rush knew the other ranchers were as eagerly scouring the country as they were. They could go back to Mundro's and wait for reports. He looked from face to face. He'd never talk them out of it. They were having too much fun.

They had been riding for fifteen minutes, when he saw Yates grab at his rifle. It was out of its scabbard before Rush saw the movement up ahead that had caught Yates' attention.

"Big old lion," Yates whispered and stood in the stirrups for a better look. "Dragging something. Probably a calf."

"I don't think so, Jim." Rush had caught a better glance at the big cat. No calf was ever gray with a reddish-gray ruff around its neck. "It's dragging a dead wolf."

"Naw," Yates said in total disbelief.

"Move forward easy," Rush advised. He thought he could show them something that would really pop their eyes. He had seen dead wolves poison lions and even bears in Mexico, and it was happening here. If Yates and the others were delighted to cross wolves off their list, wait until they could mark off a lion or two.

They moved to within plain view of the lion, and it didn't even look around.

"Acts like it's drunk," Sanders muttered.

Yates threw him a scowl. Lions were easily scared. The slightest sound would send it off in a flash.

"You can't scare that one," Rush said. "Look at its glassy eyes and the way it's staggering. He's drunk on the fumes of the poison."

"I'll be damned," Yates said softly and slid the rifle back into its boot. "He sure isn't going to let go of that wolf."

The lion was dying, but some instinct made it hang onto the easy supply of food it had found.

They followed it to where the outcropping grew more pronounced. It tried to climb to the black shadow of the cave mouth over their heads, then it collapsed. It went into horrible convulsions before it stiffened and died.

Remorseless eyes watched its final struggles. Those eyes remembered too much mangled horse flesh and dead colts.

"That cave was his home," Rush said. "I'll climb up and see what it's got there."

He peered cautiously into the shadowy interior. The female lay near the opening, her eyes dimmed in death. Three

58

dead wolves lay beside her. Her belly was swollen with young.

Rush slithered back down the hill. "They had it made. They were stocking up their food supply. She was just a few days from whelping."

He shook his head, and Yates asked, "What is it?"

"We've got a lot of poisoned meat laying around the country. We're going to lose some dogs before this is over."

It didn't bother Yates and the others. He put it for all of them, when he said, "I'll trade a few dogs for the wolves we've counted."

Heads nodded solemn agreement to his words. Sanders tried to put his gratitude into words, and he made heavy going of it.

"Rush, you've done a job. The whole county's going to be grateful—"

Rush gave him an obscene word and said, "Let's get back to the house. I imagine the others will gather there to report. You know I didn't have much breakfast. That damned Jim dragged me away before I finished."

"If he isn't the damnest one," Yates said solemnly. "I knew the minute he got back things were going to change for the better. Rush, didn't I say—"

Rush spurred away and missed the rest of it. Wasn't he and Mundro benefiting as much as anybody? Then why were they slobbering all over themselves trying to thank him?

VIII

The riders drifted in all afternoon until along about evening Mundro's yard was filled with them. And each rider brought additional elating news. Rush kept the toll on a piece of paper, and each time he called out a new total, a whoop went up from the assembled cowmen.

Mundro had kept the coffeepot going all afternoon, and finally, he stepped to the door and upended it. The lid dangled, and a few lonesome drops trickled from the pot.

"You're out of luck, Tabor," he said. "You've done drank me out of house and home." He made a lugubrious face. "I don't know what I'm going to do in the morning. I can't face the world without my cup of coffee."

"I'll ride over early in the morning and bring some," Yates promised.

"We shouldn't be drinking coffee today anyway," Sanders said. "What's the total, Rush?"

"Seventy-four," Rush answered. "If there's no duplicate counts." But even allowing for them, they had made an impresive dent in the hated predators.

Weather-beaten faces looked solemnly into weather-beaten faces, but their eyes were filled with a blazing joy. Each head was filled with the same thoughts. The number of dead wolves represented a lot of beef on the hoof, live beef that meant a few more dollars at roundup.

"You hear that?" Sanders yelled. "And Rush says there's more of them that died in the brush without making water. I say it calls for a celebration. We oughta be in town drinking something more fitting than coffee."

His words were picked up with enthusiasm, and they yelled until a man couldn't think.

Rush waited until some of that enthusiasm died. He could see why they wanted their celebration, but he could see some objections to it, also.

"Wait a minute," he said. "We've got a lot of work to do tomorrow. Do you want these dead wolves lying around your water?"

They looked at him with solemn eyes. "Are you saying we don't deserve a celebration, Rush?" Yates asked.

"I'm saying let's clean up first."

"That could take several days." The objections hit him from all sides.

"Waiting would sorta take the edge off of it," Yates wheedled.

"And none of you will be in any shape to start it tomorrow," Rush said. He wanted to sound tougher than he did. Maybe he was weakening.

"If we promise we'll get at it in the morning, no matter what."

"Oh, hell. Go ahead. I'll get started on it."

"You're going with us," a half-dozen voices said.

"Too much work—" Rush started.

Yates had a determined glint in his eyes. "You're going. If we have to tie you on your horse."

Rush looked helplessly at Mundro, and his father grinned.

"It don't look like you've got much choice," Mundro said. "Unless you figure on trying to whip all of them."

Rush looked at all of them. That would be quite a job.

"I was sorta figuring on going myself," Mundro said.

A low grin touched Rush's face. "Then I guess I'd better go to look after you." He supposed all of them had earned this. A cowman didn't have many completely worry-free days. When one did come along, it was a sin to try and dampen it.

Tabor had a pained look on his face, and Yates asked, "What are you looking so happy about?"

"I know why you're going in," Tabor said heatedly. "And maybe I agree you got a right to it. But you'd better behave yourselves. I can throw every one of you in jail."

Yates looked around at the grinning faces. "If he does, I'd say he's going to have a crowded place."

Tabor clamped his lips shut. They might have a happy time ahead of them. It didn't include him. If a bunch of drunken cowmen couldn't find trouble, they'd make it.

They hit town like a bunch of crazy Indians. They raced up and down the main street, and some of the more exuberant ones shot holes in the sky.

Tabor yelled at them until he was hoarse.

Mundro stood on the walk and watched the antics. "Sam, you're wasting your breath. They haven't done anything yet." His eyes had a reflective shine. "You're just hurting because you aren't that young."

"They haven't done anything yet but tear hell out of the peace," Tabor snapped. He tried to pull the shreds of his official dignity about him. "I'll let that pass. But you tell them I'm keeping an eye on them. One step over the line, and I'll do just as I said."

He stalked away, and Mundro's soft laugh didn't help.

The horsemen finally tied up before Wakeman's, filling the rack solidly and spilling over to the next one. They trooped in, in a body and wrestled at the door to see who would be in first.

Wakeman watched with round, apprehensive eyes.

"Quit worrying, Lud," Yates said. "You just set out the whisky. We'll give you plenty of warning so you can get out before we start tearing the place down."

He grinned at Wakeman's agonized gasp. "The first round's on me," he yelled. He saw the protest on Rush's face and chuckled. "It won't get around to me the rest of the night."

"If it does we'll have to turn you over before we can pour it down."

Yates snorted. "You quit your worrying. Haven't I always taken care of you?"

He poured both glasses full and held his up. "Here's to wolves. Dead ones."

They drank to that with enthusiasm. The evening grew to a high pitch of hilarity. They recounted over and over how the dead wolves looked, and the whisky flowed freely.

Wakeman's eyes rolled in his face at each new burst of laughter, but he never stopped pouring.

"Look at Lud," Yates said wickedly. "I'll bet he's remembering a certain night. There was only two of us then, Lud. With all of us here tonight how much faster do you think we could take your place apart?"

Wakeman threw an appealing look at Rush, and Rush said, "Jim, you're getting drunk. Slow down."

Yates gave it grave consideration. "You might be right," he agreed. He filled Rush's glass again and slapped him on the back. "And you're doing a poor job of keeping up with us."

Rush grinned. "I'm smarter than to try to keep up with you." So far, he and Mundro hadn't bought a drink, and it had worried him for a little. Then he saw the wanting to do it in their eyes. It was a small token of appreciation, and he accepted it.

He turned his head and saw Tabor standing in the doorway. Tabor beckoned with his head, and Rush said, "I'll be right back."

He moved toward Tabor, and Yates shouted after him, "If he gives you any trouble, you tell me about it."

A frown was on Rush's face. This was the third time Tabor had looked in this evening. He wondered what it would take to ease Tabor's mind. They weren't doing any harm outside of making a lot of noise.

"Step outside for a minute, Rush," Tabor said.

He had a tightness about his eyes, and it irritated Rush. Tabor was an old woman worrying about noise. He might as well accept it. He wasn't going to stop it.

"Quit stewing, Sam," he said impatiently. "I won't let them get out of hand."

Tabor's face was gloomy. "You're the boss man tonight," he agreed. "I'm glad you're not running against me for sheriff tonight. You'd win, hands down."

It restored Rush's good humor, and he laughed. "You keep that in mind, Sam, or I'll run against you."

The bantering didn't ease the tightness around Tabor's eyes, and Rush asked, "What is it?"

"Ben and Odie just left my office. They wanted to put a charge against you. They found all of their hounds dead."

Maybe Rush had more whisky than he thought for Tabor's words honed his temper. "Now, that's too goddamned bad. They were told." His anger built, and he said, "And I'm getting damned sick of you running to me yelling the Cavanaughs are in town. You run to them and tell them I'm in town. Let them keep out of my way."

The wash of light from the door showed the rising heat in Tabor's face. "All I came here was to ask you for a little help. Somebody's got to stay reasonable."

Rush ignored his plea. "All right. You asked for it."

He turned and went back inside. He cooled down fast and was ashamed of himself. He had handled Tabor rough, rougher than the situation required, but he was sick of Tabor asking him to do all of the pussyfooting. Let the Cavanaughs learn to walk a little lightly.

Yates' face was flushed, and a lot of whisky sloshed around in his belly, but he wasn't drunk. He still had enough perception to see the frown on Rush's face.

"What'd he want?" he demanded. His question was loud, and it turned heads his way.

"Nothing." Rush wished Yates was about four more whiskies down the line. Then his eyes would be too glassy to pick up little shadings in voice and face.

"Sure he did," Yates jeered. He was a persistent man when whisky prodded him. "He called you out to say nothing."

Rush swore mentally. He tried a new tack. "Aw, he was just pleased that we were keeping things down. He wanted to tell me so."

"Horse shit," Yates said, and the wicked shine in his eyes was brighter. "What are you trying to hide, Rush?"

Rush swore at the dogged insistence of Yates'. He would keep casting around until he came up with something near the truth. And the minute he guessed the Cavanaughs were in town he was just belligerent enough to go looking for them.

"Are you calling me a liar?" Rush demanded.

Behind the bar, Wakeman fluttered his hands and said, "Please, please."

Poor Lud thought a quarrel was developing. Rush grinned at him. "Don't fret, Lud. We'll take him outside." He switched his eyes to Yates. "Doesn't it always end this way?" he asked and sighed. "Jim gets a couple of drinks, and he has to be cooled off. I'd say he needs a dunking in the horse trough."

They seized on this new diversion with enthusiasm, and willing hands reached out to seize Yates.

64

Come for the filter...

A PRODUCT OF
Lorillard

KENT

WITH
THE FAMOUS MICRONITE FILTER

DELUXE LENGTH

© Lorillard 1975

...you'll stay for the taste.

DELUXE LENGTH

KENT

WITH THE FAMOUS MICRONITE FILTER

A lot of good taste that comes easy through the Micronite filter.

18 mg. "tar," 1.2 mg. nicotine av. per cigarette, FTC Report Oct. '74.

He tried to fight them off, but they overwhelmed him by sheer weight of numbers. They swarmed him to the floor, and Rush watched the pile heave and thresh about. Yates' resistance made them more determined, and Sanders panted, "Pick him up. By God, he does need cooling off."

They lifted Yates bodily from the floor, and too many hands had hold of his arms and legs for him to tear free.

Wakeman made a muted wail back of the bar, and Rush said, "Shut up, Lud. They scraped up a little sawdust. That's all."

Mundro had a frowning regard for Rush, and Rush turned his head. He couldn't fool Mundro as easily as he did the others.

Yates' arms and legs were pinioned, but he had power in his body. He heaved and jerked and twisted, making them stagger under his exertions.

His wild eyes caught Rush, and he yelled, "Damn you, Rush. This is your doing. I'll fix you for it."

Rush sighed. He wasn't fooling somebody else very well, either.

It took a time to get Yates out of the door. Just his bucking made them lose a step out of every three they took. He was swearing a blue streak as they carried him out of the door.

Rush followed them outside. Maybe he should stop it before it came to the actual dunking. But that was going to be hard to do. Yates' struggles had given them quite a mauling, and nothing was going to do now but that they dunk him. Rush was going to have a hell of a time squaring this with Yates.

Just as they started to carry him across the walk two men stepped into the light.

"Sawyer," Ben Cavanaugh shouted. "I want to talk to you."

Rush shook his head. The Cavanaughs picked the damnest times to show up. He said, "Put him down, boys."

At another time, they'd have given him an argument. Now,

they put Yates on his feet and looked at the Cavanaughs with hard, expectant eyes.

Yates didn't have all of the bad words out of his mouth, but he held them as he looked at Ben and Odie. He glanced at Rush, and quick comprehension was in his eyes.

Rush groaned. Yates always could add up pretty fair.

"So that's what Tabor told you," Yates said. "He told you they were in town. Why, you sonuvabitch. You were using me to keep attention off of them."

Rush gave him a weak grin. "Where do you get such damnfool ideas?"

Yates nodded as though he was pleased. "Yes, sir. That's it." His face had an avid shine as he looked at the faces half ringing the Cavanaughs. "It'd be a shame to take away the boys' fun after they were primed for it. Maybe we could get Ben or Odie to take my place."

Ben Cavanaugh looked from face to face with frowning uncertainty. "I got no time to play guessing games," he said. "I want to know who's going to pay for my hounds?"

"Did you lose some hounds, Ben?" Yates asked and shook his head. "Now ain't that a damned shame. Particularly, when you were warned to keep them up. We'll all sit down and cry over them with you."

"Let it go, Jim," Rush said.

Yates' face said he wasn't letting anything go. "You owe me something. Keep out of this, and maybe I'll let you off."

Rush looked at his face and sighed. Maybe Yates was right. Maybe this moment was coming to him.

"Why, you hardheaded old bastard," Yates said with deceptive softness. "You wouldn't join with the rest of us. And you get as much good out of it as any man here. But you come around and complain about some mangy hounds."

"Don't talk that way to Pa," Odie blustered.

Those hard eyes swung to him. "You figured out a way to stop me, Odie?" Yates asked.

"That's enough," Tabor said from the edge of the light. "This stops right now." He stepped into the light. "Ben, I told you, you got no claim. Now, clear out of here."

66

Yates was in a quarrelsome mood. Maybe it was the whisky, or maybe it was the memory of past abuses, but something pushed him hard.

Ben Cavanaugh was an old man, and Yates directed his remarks at Odie. "You heard him, Odie. You trail your fat butt after your old man."

"Jim, I said that's enough," Tabor said sharply.

"It's enough, if Odie wants to crawl away."

Rush was worried. Yates was biting off a big mouthful. Odie had four inches on him and maybe forty pounds of weight. If Yates kept on talking, he wouldn't leave Odie an out.

Odie's attempt at a sneer didn't ring quite true. "You can talk big, Yates. You've got enough behind you."

"Just you and me, Odie," Yates said in a purr. "But maybe that isn't fair odds to you."

Odie whipped off his hat and slammed it against the walk. "Why goddamn you."

Rush thought mournfully, *You got what you wanted, Jim.*

Yates lifted his arms from his sides. "And the gunbelt, Odie. I'm not wearing one."

Odie put a glance on his father, and Ben gave him no support. "Take it off, Odie," he ordered. "Then knock his damned head off."

Odie dropped his gunbelt and kicked it to one side.

Rush caught Tabor's arm as he started to step forward. "It's been coming for a long time, Sam. Maybe it's better happening this way."

Tabor gave him a savage glance. "If it'd end here."

It probably wouldn't, Rush thought. Regardless of who won. Things kept building up until a man couldn't believe the end results of a simple, little action.

The watchers pulled back to give Yates and Odie room. Yates circled Odie like a stalking cat, and he kept up a string of invective that drove Odie wild.

Rush shook his head. Yates looked small against that hulk.

And he was going to pay for all that lip, if Odie ever pinned him down.

The taunting pulled Odie into a bull-like charge. Yates stepped aside and speared him with a left hand on the nose. Odie squawked and threw up a hand to the hurt. The flowing blood covered it.

Rush nodded. That was the way to fight Odie. Stab him and run. Keep it up until the cumulative blows drained the strength out of Odie's legs.

The sight of Odie's blood was a spur to Yates, and he wasn't content to fight it smart. He leaped forward, intending to finish it right now, and a powerful, awkward swing caught him on the side of the head and flattened him.

Rush heard the concerted groan go up from Yates' friends, and Ben Cavanaugh roared with delight.

"Don't let him get up, Odie," he yelled. "Stomp him to pieces."

That was Odie's intention, but he wasn't fast enough. Yates rolled from under the first kick. He kept rolling until he had enough space between him and Odie to scramble to his feet.

He shook his head to clear it then said, "Come on, you lucky sonuvabitch."

Odie howled with rage and lumbered after him. Yates hit him twice while he was going away, and Odie's face showed the fresh bruises.

He expended a lot of strength trying to pin Yates down. And each charge cost him in blood or bruised flesh. He stopped, and baffled rage spread over his face. "You yellowbelly," he panted. "Stand still and fight."

Yates reacted to that, and Rush's yell was too late to stop his charge. His fists splatted against Odie's face, and he was reckless of the danger to himself. Odie's fist slid through and tagged him full on the mouth. Yates' head snapped backwards and jerked his body with it. He landed hard, and if Odie had been faster on his feet, he could've ended it there. At that Odie, landed a kick against his leg before Yates could scramble to his feet. He spat out a

68

tooth, and his face looked dazed. Every time he shook his head he sent drops of blood flying.

He backpedaled in frantic haste, and for an instant Rush had hope he was going to get clear. Then Odie reached him with a long swipe, and Yates went down again.

Odie jolted Yates with a driving kick into his side, and Rush started forward.

Tabor's outflung arm stopped him. "Yates wanted this," Tabor reminded him.

Yates caught the next kick with his hands, jerked viciously, and upended Odie.

Yates made it to his feet first. He stood on widely braced legs, his head down, his mouth open as he gasped for air. A lot had been taken out of him.

Odie hurt, too. It showed in the painful way he got back to his feet, in the way he shuffled.

"Stay clear of him, Jim," Rush yelled. That was the only way Yates could fight Odie: stand back and cut him to pieces.

But Yates acted as though his senses were scattered. He actually ran at Odie, and his face was a bloody mask. He had more strength left than Rush supposed, for he got in two good blows that rocked Odie's head.

Odie brought his fist down in an overhanded swing and caught Yates on top of the head. It pounded Yates into the dirt, and Rush thought dismally, *that's it*. For Yates' arms buckled when he tried to raise himself.

"You got him, Odie," Ben yelled in savage triumph.

But Odie was having his troubles. His chest heaved like a bellows, and he pawed at his nose and mouth as though the bleeding was clogging his breathing.

Nobody spoke as they watched Yates try to get back on his feet. He was hurt bad, and it had to be instinct, or a stubborn will forcing his screaming muscles.

He got his feet under him and hung there, half-crouched as if gathering strength for one last big effort. Then he launched himself in a dive and rammed his head into Odie's stomach.

The air exploded out of Odie, and his face twisted in agony. He stumbled backwards as Yates' weight drove into him and fell. Yates landed on top of him, and for a moment looked as helpless as Odie was. Then he clawed his way up Odie's body until he was astride his chest. He sat there and pumped in blow after blow into Odie's unprotected face.

Rush could tell when the last resistance left Odie; he could tell by the way Odie's head wobbled back and forth.

Tabor strode forward and seized Yates' shoulder. "He's out," he yelled. "Do you want to kill him?"

For a moment it looked as though Yates would fight Tabor, then a degree of sanity came into those wild eyes.

"I wouldn't mind," he said.

He tried to stand and failed the first couple of attempts. He threw off Tabor's hand and made it on his own.

He swayed drunkenly back and forth, and Rush was sure he was going to be sick. Then Yates turned and staggered to the watering trough. He thrust his head into the trough and held it under water until Rush was concerned.

He raised it and grinned feebly at Rush. "I believe I'd rather take your dunking."

"You stupid bastard," Rush raged. "Why didn't you work on his gut? He can be hurt there."

Wonderingly, Yates stared at him. "You know, I never thought of that." He plunged his head into the water again.

He looked stronger when he raised his head. And with the blood washed from his face he looked better: Not good, just better.

Odie still lay in the street, and Yates shook his head. He found his hat, dipped it full, then carried it to Odie. His step looked almost steady.

"Odie gets more damned baths this way," he said and poured the water into Odie's face.

Odie groaned and rocked his head. He blew out a sputtering breath, and his one good eye opened. The other was closed tight.

It took a lot of vague staring for him to get his bear-

70

ings. He settled on the face hanging over him, and it all came back to him. He tried to get up, and the strength wasn't there.

"I'll kill you for this," he said in a harsh whisper.

"You do that," Yates said cheerfully.

Ben Cavanaugh screamed in impotent rage, and a man had to listen hard to get any sense out of his words. He wanted Yates arrested, he wanted him thrown in jail for the rest of his life.

"What for?" Tabor said. "It was a fair fight. You wouldn't be screaming if Odie was the one on his feet."

Disgust washed across his face. "You wouldn't listen to me. You had to lean on this. You and Odie get out of town. And if you don't think I mean it, try me."

He looked at Yates and growled, "Did you prove anything?"

Yates gave it careful thought. "I proved I can hurt in a hell of a lot of places at once." He looked around, and though grinning was painful he made it. "I think I earned a drink. Who's going to buy me one?"

Everybody offered. Everybody but Ben Cavanaugh. He was having too tough a job getting Odie on his feet.

IX

Rush stood on a ladder and nailed the board into place. A half-dozen more, and that gaping hole in the barn's side would be covered. As he took another one Mundro handed up, he said, "I wonder if Jim's moving any better this morning."

Mundro shook his head. "I'll say one thing for him. He never quit. Those first two mornings after the fight must've been hell for him."

Rush could agree to that. Yates had insisted upon doing his share of the work in disposing of the dead wolves.

"It's a hell of a way for men to settle their differences," Mundro said.

"You carry a few marks yourself," Rush jeered.

"That was when I was younger and didn't have any brains," Mundro said calmly. "I still say it's a hell of a way."

Rush pondered it as he drove in the nails. Mundro was probably right. But damnit, sometimes a man couldn't keep out of a fight.

Mundro pushed another board up, and Rush checked his reach for it. "Somebody coming," he announced.

That slight form wasn't any man. His heart picked up an uneven thump. He couldn't see her features plainly yet, and he must be imagining things. But the lift of her head, the way she handled herself said that was Julia. He must be light-headed from being out in the sun too long. What would she be doing riding way over here?

Mundro shaded his eyes and peered toward the approaching rider. "It's Julia Mauer."

It hit Rush hard that he didn't even know her last name. But how did Mundro know it?

Mundro had a malicious twinkle in his eyes. "Don't you remember her? Mauer had the place a couple of miles from us. She used to follow you around. She was about twelve or thirteen, all legs and big eyes. You used to call her the tagalong nuisance."

He grinned at the shading of color in Rush's face. "Maybe you can call her that again and get rid of her."

Rush's swearing increased in direct proportion to Mundro's laughter. He remembered it all now. Mauer couldn't make it here and had moved to Ontario. He couldn't let Mundro see his elation, and he'd never call her a tagalong again. He guessed there were certain ages in a man's life when he didn't know when he was well off.

He climbed down and was rubbing his hands on his pants when she rode up. He guessed he was grinning like an idiot, but he couldn't help it.

72

"Hello, Julia," Mundro said and extended his hand in welcome.

Her laughter made a man feel good. "Mundro, you knew me." She exchanged a conspiratorial glance with him. "He didn't."

"I did, too," Rush protested.

"Besides being blind he's a poor liar," Mundro said, and Julia went into gales of laughter.

"If you don't let up on me, I'll never forgive you," Rush growled.

She placed her hand on his arm. "Rush, I'm sorry. But if you knew how you looked trying to make me believe that lie. I guess I have changed a little." She had dimples and a wicked glint in her eyes.

He felt all hollow inside. It was crazy how fast a man's life could change. He felt as though all the solid ground had dropped from beneath his feet.

"A little," he admitted sheepishly. "I guess you knew me."

"The moment I saw you," she said promptly.

"Don't let him suffer, Julia," Mundro said dryly. "Tell him that women are just naturally smarter than men."

"Why, Mundro. I thought we kept that pretty well hidden."

Mundro laughed. "Only until we get so old the learning of it doesn't do us any good."

He slipped his hand under her arm. "Come in, and I'll make you a cup of the worst coffee you ever tasted."

They walked ahead of Rush, and he scowled at his father's back. They acted as though an old and valued friendship was between them. Were they this close when she lived around here? He couldn't remember, or he hadn't been interested enough to notice.

Mundro made the coffee and handed her a cup. He grinned as she took a cautious sip. "Did I lie to you?"

"I'm trying to remember," she answered. "I think once before I tasted coffee that was worse."

73

"And all along I thought I had the championship," Mundro said mournfully.

She did something to a room. She filled it with light and gaiety, and Rush thought, she'll always have that quality.

"How's your folks?" Mundro asked.

A momentary sadness touched her face. "Father died three years ago. Mother a year after." She dwelt in the sad past a moment longer, then pushed it from her.

Neither Rush or Mundro said they were sorry. She knew that. She was a stayer, Rush thought. Things might bowl her over, but they couldn't keep her that way. It was a fine quality in either man or woman.

"Rush," she said. "I rode over to tell you something that might be important. A British Major brought some clothes in to be laundered. I thought I couldn't keep my face straight while he talked. His accent and some of the words he used." She mimicked the major with a fair degree of success, and broad grins were on Mundro and Rush's faces.

"Oh," Julia said in quick dismay. "I just thought of something. I wonder if he had trouble keeping his face straight while I talked."

They looked at each other solemnly, and Rush said, "That's something to think about, all right."

He waited for her to pick up her story. She had to have a reason to tell him about a British major.

"He's over here to buy horses for the British army," she continued. "They need them for some war they're fighting in Africa. He's interested in the slick-ears."

"The oreanas?" Rush asked incredulously.

She nodded. "He says he'll buy all he can get. And Rush—" She had to catch her breath. "He'll pay forty dollars a piece for them green broke."

Rush stared at her then shook his head. "You talked to a crazy man."

"Don't you go making any snap judgments," Mundro said. He had a shine in his eyes. When a man multiplied forty

74

dollars times all the oreanas that were running around loose, the resulting sum made him giddy.

"You ought to talk to him, Rush," Julia said.

Rush drew a deep breath. "I'm going to. I'm just scared to believe in it too much." He pushed back from the table and stood. "Can you leave right now?"

Rush looked back from the door. Mundro's eyes were absorbed in something far away, and Rush knew what he looked at—a little extra money to build and repair, money to give them a breathing space.

"Don't get your hopes up too high," he said.

Mundro started guiltily. "It's all right to dream a little bit, isn't it?"

"Sure," Rush said gently.

Major Whitmore was a slight man looking dapper in his well-fitting uniform. He had blond hair and a neatly trimmed line of mustache. His clipped speech sounded odd, and it was easy to fall into the trap of thinking here wasn't much man—until you looked at his eyes. They were pale blue and about as direct as any eyes Rush had looked into. Whitmore was out of his element here. Rush would bet he cut a hell of a swath in his own.

"The young lady said she knew just the man for the job," Whitmore said. "Can you do it?"

Julia was right about that odd accent. Rush didn't know what Whitmore did to words, but he sure said them different.

"How many do you want?" He'd be sick if the major said ten or a dozen.

"All you can deliver," Whitmore answered. "I thought you chaps knowing the country could do a better job than I could."

It was hard to keep your face straight when you were filled with joy, when it hammered at your lips for escape.

"Any specifications?" Rush asked.

"Eight-hundred pound ponies. Four and five years old."

75

Rush nodded. The major wanted full mouths. "Julia said you wanted them green broke."

Whitmore smiled showing good teeth. "At least, ridden once or twice."

"Any special color?"

Whitmore shook his head. "Whatever they run." He rubbed his hands together. "If I can get what I want, we'll bloody well teach those stubborn beggars a lesson."

Rush's expression said he didn't understand, and Whitmore explained. "We're in a war in South Africa. With the Boers."

Rush shook his head. He'd never heard of them.

"Farmers. Dutch and Huguenot descent. Hardheaded people, but they'll jolly well learn."

Rush felt an instinctive pity for them. The war was probably over land, and he always lined up with the man who was fighting for his land. But it wasn't his war, and it was too far away to carry much emotional impact. He thought with grim humor that when those English soldiers tried to ride those wild oreanas, they'd get more casualties from the horses than they'd ever suffer from the Boers.

He stood and said, "As long as you keep buying, I'll keep delivering."

Whitmore gave him that firm grip again. "I'll depend on you, old chap. You'll keep in touch with me?"

"It won't be tomorrow," Rush said and smiled.

"Understand that, old chap." That was testiness in Whitmore's voice. "Been around horses all my life."

He shook Rush's hand again. He wasn't angry. He just wanted to keep the record straight.

Outside his door, Rush stared at Julia. "I wasn't dreaming, was I?" he said.

He reached out in sudden exuberance and hugged her. At the moment he was too elated to realize there wasn't the slightest struggle in her.

"Julia, do you know what this means? I can get the ranch fixed up. I can put it back on a paying basis." He held her at arms' length. "And you made it all possible."

Her lips were slightly parted, and they looked so moist

and inviting. Her eyes were big and shimmering, and it would be easy for a man to drown himself in them.

He hadn't the slightest idea of kissing her, but there he was with his lips on hers. And the promise of them was very real. They quivered in acceptance then firmed with an equal demand.

He lifted his head and looked at her in awe. Something had just clubbed him over the head, and he would take that kind of clubbing for the rest of his life. His voice came out as a shaky squeak, and he had to breathe deeply before he could steady it.

"Julia," he said in wonder. "I think I'm falling in love with you."

"I know," she said softly.

He frowned. How did she know? He'd just discovered it himself.

An impish delight danced in her eyes. "Don't worry about it. Didn't Mundro say women are smarter than men? At least, they know where they're going."

He pulled her back to him. He'd have to punish her good. He wouldn't let her get her breath at all this time.

X

THE COWMEN and their hands squatted in a semicircle about Rush. Thirty men were at least interested in hearing what he had to say. He finished telling them about Whitmore, and there wasn't a word. Nobody could pry a thought out of those leathery faces if they wanted to hide it. Rush knew them well, but even he was disappointed at the absolute lack of reaction. Some of them picked up handfuls of dirt and let it sift through their fingers. Others flicked pebbles at imaginary targets, while a few rolled fresh smokes.

They had listened attentively, for his success with the wolves had given his ideas standing. He appreciated that, but he wished some of them would say something. He was wise not to say anything further for a man could oversell an idea. But damnit, he expected more support than this. Even Yates squatted there blowing his breath out softly.

The damned hardhead, Rush thought irritably. Give him a wild idea with no practicality in it, and he'd plunge into it hell for breakfast. But dangle something solid before him, and he had to walk all around it and look it over from every angle.

"Were you drunk when you talked to this major?" Dave Johnson asked.

"I wasn't drunk," Rush snapped.

"One of you had to be. Forty dollars for a slick-ear." Johnson snorted at the absurdity of the whole thing.

"That was his offer." Rush was getting hot in the neck at their attitude.

"It'd take some time," Oley Parsons said thoughtfully. "And a lot of hard riding. A man could bust a good horse all to pieces trying to catch one little knothead."

Rush glared at him. Certainly, it'd take time and effort. Did they expect to be just handed something?

"Did you see the color of his money?" Yates asked with a stern face.

"He didn't see the color of our oreanas, either," Rush shouted. "Did you expect him to pay in advance?" He was building a real good mad at them, and it was fueled by the sick disappointment welling up in him. This had seemed such a golden chance, but it'd take all of them to handle it.

"He builds up steam real easy," Yates said and looked solemnly at the faces around.

Rush saw something he had missed before: the twinkle in their eyes. They were baiting him, and he'd walked in and snapped up every morsel offered him.

"You bastards," he said helplessly.

They were on their feet mauling him, buffeting him with elbows and heels of palms. They spun him from one pair

78

of hands to another, and each gave its quota of punishment. The excitement was alive in their faces, and they laughed and shouted with it.

When they finally eased up on him he said breathlessly, "I'd rather have enemies any day than you."

"What'd I tell you?" Yates said softly. "The minute he came back everything changed for the better. He's our luck piece."

That worried Rush a little. It placed a big burden on him. If something went wrong, he would be responsible for the following disappointment.

"You done any figuring, Rush?" Sanders asked.

"I figure we'll try for a small gather. Say fifty or sixty head. Then we'll go look at the color of Whitmore's money. If he wants more, we can get them for him. I figure we can do it in a week. That's all we'll lose."

Heads bobbed in solemn agreement. That was the one thing they had to spend in abundance—time.

None of them minimized the size of the job ahead of them. They had to dig a handful of wild horses out of four hundred and fifty square miles of desert rimrock country, as rough a country as a man ever rode over. And there would be no picking of trails. They'd be in full run just to keep in sight of the oreanas, and at breakneck speed they'd come off cliffs that just walking down would dry up the spit in a man's mouth.

"There they are," Yates said, pointing to a distant band, small enough to look like dots.

"Put a lump of sugar in your hand and walk up to them," Dave Johnson said.

Rush wished it was that easy. In the summer, the herds of wild horses drifted up to the heights among the cliff shadows. A cow brute ranged the lower country, but the oreanas liked it high up, where they could look around. Right now, he'd bet those distant dots all had their heads up and pointed this way. And the stallion would be on the highest point. If the riders started to break down that distance between

79

them, the stallion would whistle, and the whole bunch would take off around the shellrock rims, climbing the benches with as much sureness of foot as a mountain goat.

And they could fly. Rush had seen bunches, running like antelopes over over the hard floor of a canyon, their tough hooves setting up an echo that slammed back and forth between the canyon walls. At times, their own echo seemed to scare them into renewed speed. A canyon was a huge sounding board, magnifying noise until a man's head rang with it. The oreana had every advantage: his natural wariness, hooves and legs toughened by running in this country, and the biggest one of all, his familiarity with every gap and pass in the country. If a man ran them for fun, he wasn't too disappointed in lack of results. This was different. This had the smell of money in it.

Every eye was intent on the distant dots, and every head was filled with the same thoughts.

"This won't get it done," Rush said breaking the spell. They had a lot of work to do before they could run an oreana a foot, and they'd better be getting at it.

Rush set up his main camp at Three Fingers Butte. Later when the oreanas grew wary from pursuit, he would scatter smaller spike camps through the breaks so that he could move the operation from place to place conserving his horse flesh.

It made a large camp. They had forty extra horses and a chuck wagon. Old Lucas Martin would do the cooking, dragging his game leg and swearing at the remarks directed at his food. Rush had heard him yell half a hundred times,

"Complain your damned heads off. But I notice every one of you turn in an empty plate."

Tonight, Lucas' harassment would start again. The riders would use the hoary old jokes, swearing they'd dump the food out on the ground, but even the buzzards wouldn't eat it. And Lucas would cuss and stomp around. He never seemed to get wise to the ribbing, or maybe he enjoyed it as much as the riders did. And even though he wouldn't put a boot outside of camp his share would be the same as the others.

The meal was over, and they sat or stretched out around the campfire in weary contentment. This was the good part of the day, with its work all wrapped up so that a man could ease his tired bones without guilt.

"Lucas," Yates called. "You got any baking soda? I swear if I could get a horse to buck like my belly, nobody could stick on it."

A chuckle ran around the fire at the choice oaths Yates received in return.

"You know that box canyon near Yellow Jacket Springs?" Rush asked. He picked up a stick and drew in the dust. "It's narrow near its end, and we'll only have to fence one way. Maybe a couple of swinging gates will be wide enough to span it. We'll see when we get there." He drew more lines. "That country is sloping, and a dozen little canyons lead out of it. We'll string a wire across the mouth of those little canyons and attach strips of canvas to them. The wind flapping the strips should stop the oreanas from breaking out of the drive."

Heads nodded approval. It was good planning. Those flapping tatters would save manpower. They wouldn't have to station a rider at each canyon mouth to turn the wild ones.

"We'll get busy tomorrow and build our trap and string our wires," Rush said. He looked around him. "Anybody got any improvements?"

Yates shook his head. "Can't think of a thing, Rush." His gesture was picked up all around the fire.

It took two days to build the big trap corral. They cut long poles and packed them with brush until a pack rat would have to do some hunting to find a place through. Some of the posts couldn't be set because of the rocky ground, and those had to be braced with rock piled high on all sides of the post. They made the swinging gates using wire as the hinges and stretching a length of wire tight between

81

the top of the tall gate post and the end of the gate so that its lifting effect would keep the gate from dragging.

Rush tested it and nodded. The gate swung nice and easy. If they got the oreanas this far, a rider could jump off and throw the gates shut behind them. He wished it was swinging shut on a bunch right now. Between now and the actual happening was many a mile.

He couldn't help but worry about the coming drive. What had he left undone? Was there some little gap that he didn't know about and had failed to cover? He could bet the wild ones knew about it. The whole drive could filter right out of their hands through some little old ten-foot gap that was brush-screened from view.

"I guess we're ready to take a ride in the morning," he said. He'd made his throw. But the dice were still spinning. He couldn't read them yet.

"Maybe we'll scoop up Starshell," Yates said.

That started an argument. Most of the men said the horse was a legend, that he didn't exist. He had been built out of imagination, and his fabulous speed and endurance was something out of mens' minds. He ran the biggest band in the breaks, and his mares were the fastest and strongest.

"Goddamn it, I know what I'm talking about," Yates said. "I saw him once. He must've had over two hundred head in his bunch."

A couple of other voices backed him up that the stallion existed, a big, lightning-fast devil with a deep bay coat like burnished fire.

Rush couldn't join in the talk. He had never seen the animal. He might be real, but Rush leaned more to the side of legend. They were still arguing about it, when he crawled into his blankets.

Riders slipped out of camp long before the faintest suggestion of dawn was in the sky. But they had a way to go, and night riding would make it slow. Some of them cut off to take up strategic positions along the flanks of the drive, popping out to scare the broomtails back onto a fairly straight course toward the trap. The unexpected appearance of a man could stop a swerving before it became a full-fledged break. The actual horse runners wouldn't move until light.

They made a wide swing to the long ridge running between Steamboat and Runaway, and when they reached it, the country stretched out wide and big before them.

Somebody yelled, "There they go," and the spaced line of riders were instantly in a gallop.

The mustangs were a good mile ahead of them already in full flight, and the early sun picked up fire from the stallion's coat in the lead. For a moment Rush's throat was tight as he thought, *It's Starshell.* Despite a man's disbelief he always hedged his bet by thinking there might be truth in the legend. Then his throat eased. If that was Starshell, legend had built him up out of proportion. That stallion was ordinary sized, and he had less than a hundred head behind him.

They had the bunch running straight at the canyon trap. The faster ones were beginning to stream ahead running bunched up, with the gaps growing greater between them and the laggards.

Each man's mouth was stretched wide with his yelling, and it helped push the horses ahead of them.

Twice, Rush saw the wire-strung canvas turn them at gaps, and another time Oley Parsons did a hell of a job cutting an angle to turn them toward the right.

They poured down off of the ridge riding at top speed dropping lower through the breaks, over rocks, boulders and sand dunes, anything a man could get his horse over. The wind whipped a man's face, and the brush lashed his legs. He felt its stinging even through his chaps. He didn't dare think about his course. All he could hope for was that his horse didn't step into a hole or trip over a rock. If a horse went down at this reckless speed, about the best a man could hope for was a broken bone—and he prayed it wasn't his neck.

They covered ground, and the wild herd held to a fairly

83

straight line. A half-dozen times Rush saw them cut toward the mouth of a canyon or gap that would lead them back safely into the hills, and each time a rider showed himself, hollering and waving his hat. And each time, the stallion in the lead swerved back onto course.

The oreanas weren't running with the earlier, wild abandonment. The relentless pursuit was beginning to sap them, and the pace was slowing. But the domestic horses were suffering equally.

They had about a mile to go, Rush judged, until they hit the mouth of the box canyon. If they could keep them traveling this way for that little distance, they had them.

The line of the horse runners began to bend at the ends forming a half-circle. And like a net it drew tighter and tighter until the only way the oreanas could escape the closing trap was to try to break back through the line pressing them.

Rush thought several of them were going to attempt it. The stallion, in particular, didn't like the opening of the trap canyon. He whirled, his head flung high, and Rush was close enough to see the muddy, rolling eyes and the red flare of its nostrils. It hung there uncertainly, and the mares wheeled and bunched around it. This was the bad moment. If the stallion had enough nerve to break through the gaps between the riders, the mares would follow him. And a lot of them would make it. Rush had seen other drives ruined in this vital moment.

He yelled with renewed vigor and flailed his hat, and riders on both siders were doing the same. The stallion's nerve broke, and he wheeled again, bounding forward toward the canyon opening. The dig of his hooves tore out brush by its roots.

They poured into the canyon, and Rush yelled in sheer jubilation, they had them now. All they had to do was to follow them in and swing the gates shut.

He and Yates were the first to reach the gates. They hauled on the reins and jumped at the same time, and the momentum of their mounts carried them forward in several running, staggering steps.

Rush grabbed one gate, Yates the other. They swung them together in wild haste though the immediate need was gone. The oreanas would run to the base of the far wall and would mill there before they came back.

They put wire after wire on the two gates, binding them tightly together, and only then did they stop to pant and grin at each other.

"We got over a hundred," Yates said.

Rush knew Yates was multiplying a hundred times forty. "Some of them won't fit."

"Hell, I forgot. But it'll still be a lot of money."

Rush could agree to that. He listened to the screaming, tearing fight of a couple of stallions in the corral. They ran together in harmony enough outside, but put them in a confined place, and they went at each other. There was some parallel with human behavior in that, but he was too tired to pin it down.

He was surprised to see how much of the day had gone. Some of the men wanted to start work on the oreañas right away, and Rush decided against it. Men and horses were tired, and a night might settle the oreanas down a little.

"We'll move camp," he said, "and start in the morning."

They started early in the morning, and several days of hard work lay ahead of them. They cut out the aged and the very young first, and Yates' face grew longer each time the gates swung open to release another one. Rush knew what he was thinking. There went another forty dollars. The undersized went next, and then Rush started a more restricted culling, paying particular attention to the individual. A man kept alert every minute he was among the mustangs. If he didn't, he'd find himself with a broken head, or at least, spitting out his teeth.

Yates started to put a loop on a stallion, and Rush yelled, "Watch him."

The stallion reared and walked on his hind legs striking

85

out with his forehooves like a man boxing. Yates ducked one of the flailing forehooves and turned a scared face toward Rush.

"We don't want him," Rush said. "He's got a killer look in his eyes. He shows his teeth like a snarling dog. And look at the way the hair on his neck turns the wrong way. A man couldn't be watchful enough to be safe around him. He'll wait for his time, and he'll kill somebody."

Yates put a speculative look on him, and Rush grinned. "I learned a little about horses while I was in Mexico."

"Whose arguing with you?" Yates asked.

They cut out the stallion and followed him with any horse with a hammer head, a set of bad ears, or a vicious eye. He threw out all the narrow-headed ones, like those two pin-eared mares. When Yates protested at the elimination of some of them, Rush said, "Whitmore would only throw them out. I believe he knows his horses."

Yates tried to count the remaining ones and swore every time he lost count. It was difficult to be accurate when a band kept constantly shifting. Finally, he said, "I make it sixty-three."

Rush nodded. He made it the same count. He grinned as he asked, "How many bumps do you think you have ahead of you?"

Yates groaned. Each one of the oreanas had to be over-powered and ridden several times. Even then they'd be a far way from being gentle. Riders would limp to the chuck wagon for their evening meal, and they'd be damned lucky if they didn't have broken bones.

Rush topped the first one, a sorrel mare. She fought well for a few seconds then it ran swiftly out of her. She stood there blowing hard, and she only quivered when he ran his hand soothingly along her neck. She was going to break easy. Another ride would probably do it.

Some of the fights were vicious and prolonged, and the canyon rang with oaths from the riders and whoops of delight from the watchers. Men went down, and some scrambled to their feet running painfully. Others lay there for a few

86

seconds, a dazed look on their faces. Then an enraged animal had to be hazed away from them.

That night, Lucas cackled maliciously at the stiff movements and the groans that weren't made but were still there behind locked lips.

"Come on," he said. "Come on. Where's all the smart-alec remarks tonight?"

Yates put a baleful eye on him. "If I could get up, I'd kill him," he said.

They cut a day off of Rush's estimate of the breaking time. When they were finished, he said, "Take them to Ontario, Jim."

Yates looked surprised. "You're not going?"

Rush shook his head. He wanted to go. He wanted to see Julia. But he could make time by staying here. "I want to look over the land," he said. "I want to locate a bigger bunch."

He started to turn away, then stopped. "You bring back every dime of that money," he ordered.

It was hard for a bruised man to be cheerful. "I hope he pays it," Yates said gloomily.

XI

LUCAS STAYED with Rush in camp. He served breakfast and grumbled, "I don't know how to cook for just two men. Damned if I don't kinda miss them." He glared at Rush. "Don't you go telling them that."

Rush laughed as he mounted. "You're a fake, Lucas. But I'll keep your secret."

He had no definite destination in mind. He climbed higher and higher, every now and then stopping to scan the country with glasses. He saw several bunches of oreanas, but they were small in number. He wanted to spot a big bunch and familiarize himself with their range and habits. He didn't expect to see the big red stallion, but the horse stuck in his mind. Yates swore he'd seen him, and there'd been a difference in his tone. Usually, Rush could tell when Yates was spinning a yarn.

He headed for the high peak ahead. He paused to let Wrangle drink from the water hole at its base, and its edges were chopped up by countless hoofprints. Hard excitement started in him. This looked like the range of a big bunch.

He let Wrangle pick its pace as he headed for the crest. Its pinnacle would give him a vast sweep of the country. The wild horses used this peak, for their hooves had beaten out a well-defined path.

He made a hairpin turn, and there looking him right in the eye was a red stallion. For a few seconds, Rush and the horse were locked in mutual surprise. It had to be Starshell, and the sight of the animal would make a horseman go all soft inside. He was big and deep-chested, and he had long, clean legs. It had wide-spaced, intelligent eyes, and it carried its head with a proud lift. The stallion was no legend. He was real. He was there in the flesh right in front of Rush.

He let out a yell he couldn't hold, and Starshell snorted and whirled. The oreanas, bunched up behind him, whirled at the same time, and their hooves clattered and pounded at the rocky path. By the time a man blinked twice they were gone.

Rush sat there in a trance. By God, would he have something to tell the others when they got back. His eyes widened at the sudden thought. Wouldn't it be something if he could show them. He could see the way their eyes would widen and the way their mouths would drop open. The thought was like reaching for the moon. How could a single man catch Starshell? He had probably gotten as close to him a moment ago as he would ever get. Somebody had given the stallion a fanciful name, and it fitted him.

He urged Wrangle on, wanting another glimpse of the band.

He had been so enthralled he hadn't even gotten an estimate of how many horses were in the bunch.

He climbed to the crest and searched the country with glasses slowly and thoroughly. He never saw a glimpse of them. It was impossible for them to get down off the peak this fast and disappear, but they had. Of course, he could've imagined the whole thing. He grinned at the thought. Nobody could tell him he hadn't seen Starshell.

He turned back toward the camp. He could search the rest of the day and never see a hair of them. But those prints around the water hole said it was a favorite watering spot. He knew a piece of their range.

"I found my bunch," he said in answer to Lucas' question. To all other questions he shook his head.

"You talk a man's arm off," Lucas snorted and limped away.

At the end of four days, Rush thought he had established a pattern for Starshell's bunch. They watered at dawn, then grazed aimlessly before they moved up the peak. It took them better than an hour to climb to the crest, then they disappeared down over the other side. He took the glasses from his eyes and rubbed them. A nebulous plan was taking shape in his head, so impractical that he knew it couldn't work. He would have one chance, and he would have to be shot with luck, if it succeeded. When he thought of all the things he had to have working for him, he groaned in despair. But he could think of nothing else. Starshell would never be run down. The horse knew every foot of the country, and he was too canny to make a mistake. One cast, Rush thought, and that's it. And his chances of crapping out were far greater than of throwing a seven.

He rode back to the camp and sat out the rest of the day in thoughtful silence.

"Damn it," Lucas complained. "I might as well be alone."

Rush wanted to talk to him about it, but he wouldn't be able to stand the growing incredulity in Lucas' eyes; he didn't want to hear him say, "Man, you've plumb lost your head."

He left the camp shortly after midnight. He carried with

him a short hand ax and three lassos. On the way, he stopped and cut a four-foot length of six-inch log, then whittled a channel in the middle of it—a channel deep enough to hide the rope in, so that when the log was dragged the rope wouldn't fray. It was an awkward thing to carry, and Wrangle didn't like it, snorting his displeasure. Rush swore at him and kicked him sharply, and Wrangle decided he had to accept the burden.

He reached the water hole with less than an hour left before sunup. It was enough time, but he couldn't fool around. He dumped the log, the hand ax and the ropes, then rode Wrangle a good half-mile away. He wished he could have used him, but sure as hell Wrangle would bugle at the smell of the wild ones, and they'd be in full flight before Rush could begin to move.

He tethered the horse securely, then walked back cursing the rocks that turned under his boots. He worked feverishly now. He'd rather have time to wait than be caught before he was prepared.

He ran the loop in one of the lassos down small and slipped it over the log. He ran his fingers over the whittled channel and could barely feel the rope. He put a knot in the rope down tight against the loop so that it couldn't loosen and flip off of the log. He knotted two ropes together, testing the knot over and over for holding power. The false light of dawn was diluting the darkness when he carried the log and ropes into the thickest part of the brush at the east side of the hole. The other four mornings, the oreanas came in from the west, and the rising sun was full in their eyes. If they changed pattern, he was lost. He tested the wind and nodded. So far, his luck was holding. He would be downwind from them. Upon sudden impulse, he scooped up handfuls of mud and smeared them on his hands, face, and clothing. He didn't know that it would do any good, but it might help keep his scent down.

He moved back to the brush and coiled the rope carefully. Then he hunkered down and waited. Now, all of the imponderables hit him, and he groaned under their weight.

He had noticed that the mares stopped and drank immediately, but the stallion always made a circuit of the water hole as though checking everything before it drank. If Starshell changed that this morning because of some animal whim, Rush was dead. At the best he would have a couple of seconds in his favor, and that was asking for everything.

The light strengthened, and the worries assailed him. Suppose they didn't come here this morning; suppose they had grazed so far yesterday that they would pick a closer water hole. He stuck the knives of doubt into him as the rim of the sun showed, then climbed slowly higher. *It's not going to go,* he thought miserably then he heard the click of a hoof against stone.

He wanted to flatten against the ground, but he had to have his feet under him. All he could do was to make his breathing as shallow and spaced as he could.

He kept his face averted and listened to the noisy suck of the horses drinking. When he dared a peek, the stallion was halfway around the hole on its usual round. But it was uneasy this morning as though it sensed something wrong. Every couple of steps it'd throw up its head and nicker nervously.

A little closer, Rush prayed. Just a little bit more.

He watched the stallion move a couple of more feet. He wished the margin could have been cut more, but he couldn't risk it. The horse was definitely more nervous. At any moment it could wheel and break into full flight.

He sucked in breath for the biggest yell he would ever make in his life. That had to have been a horrible apparition that burst out of the brush almost in the stallion's face. It held him for that vital split-second, and Rush made his throw. If he ever had to make a good one, this was it.

The moment it took the loop to settle about the horse's neck was surely a hundred years long. All around, the oreanas were whistling in shrill fright and breaking into a mad run. Starshell bolted, and the rope tightened. It hissed as it

91

streaked out of its coils, and Rush jumped aside to keep from being hit by the log.

He stood there not believing it. He had a rope around the stallion's neck, and the log would act as a drag slowing it down. The battle wasn't over, but he'd taken a big step.

He turned and ran for Wrangle. That log should drag quite a path through the brush. It shouldn't be hard to follow.

By the time he reached Wrangle he breathed, and he fought the knot in the reins. He forced himself to settle down. A few more seconds weren't going to make any difference. He swung into the saddle and spurred back to the water hole.

It didn't take much tracking ability to follow the stallion's path. That bouncing log chewed out clumps of grass and small brush. Even when it was riding smooth, it left small furrows in the ground. Rush saw a couple of places where it had become entangled in denser brush, and the horse had to fight it free.

At that, it took the better part of an hour for Rush to come within sight of it. Its head wasn't carried as high, and it seemed leg weary. None of the bunch was in view, but that didn't matter. This was the one Rush wanted.

It saw Rush and put on a burst of speed, and the log bounced and skipped along behind it. There was a big risk of the log catching and throwing the stallion, breaking its neck or a leg, but Rush would never get his hands on him any other way.

He could have caught up with it, but he kept behind it running the last of its strength out of it.

The log lodged in brush, and Starshell gave a feeble tug on it then stood with drooping head. It had ripped the log out of worse entanglements, but now it was thoroughly exhausted.

It didn't even raise its head very much as Rush rode within roping distance. He dropped another loop around its neck, and it squealed in momentary frenzy and made a weak run at Wrangle. It was easy for Wrangle to skip out of the way, and when the log put pressure on the rope, the stallion stopped.

Rush kept trying to provoke other rushes from it and decided it was dead beat. He set Wrangle to holding him, knowing Wrangle would keep the rope taut. He stepped out of the stirrup, keeping a wary eye on Starshell. The animal moved, and Wrangled moved with it, holding it easily. Wrangle couldn't have begun to hold it if it had been fresh.

Rush walked around the stallion. He yelled a couple of times and threw up his hands. Starshell flinched, but that was all. Rush decided he could safely cut the log free. He made a swipe with his knife and only Wrangle held the stallion.

He ran back to the saddle prepared for anything. He moved Wrangle, putting force on the rope, and he had to drag the horse, then it moved with the pressure on legs that quivered with exhaustion.

Rush kept a careful eye behind him, anticipating at any time an enraged squeal and a rush at him. But the log drag had done its work too thoroughly. There was no strength left in Starshell for a charge.

Rush's heart was singing as he rode into camp. Lucas stared in total disbelief, and Rush gave him a gay flip of his hand as he led Starshell past him.

He closed and wired the gates behind him before he flipped the loop off Starshell's neck. He would have to open to lead Wrangle out, but he was taking no chances there might be a dash left in Starshell. He would have to have help before he freed the loop of the trailing rope.

Starshell stood there in dull defeat, not realizing the restraint was gone. Its head came up slowly, and it bugled, but it was only a weak imitation of its former volume. It stared at Rush, then turned and moved away, putting as much distance as it could between it and the man.

Rush led Wrangle through the gates and rewired them. Only then did he let down, and the full awareness of how tired he was hit him. His legs trembled, and his hands shook

93

as he tried to roll a cigarette. He made a bad job of it and tossed it on the ground.

Lucas limped toward him. "How'd you do it?" he demanded.

"How'd I do what?" Rush's face was innocent.

Lucas hopped up and down in his rage. "Rush, if you don't talk to me now, I'll—I'll—" He spluttered with his effort of finding something drastic enough.

Rush threw his arm across the old man's shoulders. "I'll tell you all about it, Lucas. If you don't say anything to the others when they get back."

Lucas grinned in understanding. "Sorta of a surprise, huh? All you'll do to them is knock their eyes out."

XII

THE OTHERS came in before noon the following day. Rush looked at Yates' sober face and knew alarm. He had expected to see them skylarking around, and all of them had the same gloomy look.

"What went wrong? Didn't he want them?"

Yates shook his head. "He was pretty mad, Rush. He said he told you what he wanted. You didn't meet a single specification."

"Why, damn him," Rush said wrathfully. "He's a liar."

He stopped as he saw the grin growing on Yates' face. Then they were all laughing and hooting at him.

"I ought to flatten every one of you," he said.

Yates backed, his hands held out in mock pleading. "I'll talk, Rush. Just give me a chance."

Rush grinned in spite of himself. "You damned fool."

"He only rejected three," Yates said. "He was tickled to death with them. And he wants more just as soon as we

94

can get them." He pulled a wad of bills, thick enough to choke a cow, from his pants pocket. "He gave me a draft on the bank, and I had it cashed into twenties. My God, did you ever see so much money in your life?"

He handed the bills to Rush, and there was defiance in his face. "I sold the three rejects for ten dollars apiece. We drank it up. I figure we had it coming. If you don't think so, take it out of my share."

"You had it coming," Rush agreed. Man, he held a hatful of money. He unfolded the bills and said, "Come and get it."

Every face had a hungry, expectant shine. This was cash money, money that didn't come out of the meager resources of the ranch. This was a fresh breath, and there was more where this came from.

Each man received an equal share. Layton and his three sons got the most because they had four shares, and Rush didn't begrudge them a dime. He and Mundro had a hundred and sixty dollars, and they could do a lot with that much.

He grinned as he watched them hold and look at the money.

Lucas was bursting with impatience to talk, and Rush shook his head in warning at him.

"You'd better put that in your pockets," he said, "before you rub the numbers off of it." He made his voice very casual. "Do you know we left one head in the corral?"

"You're crazy," Yates protested, and a dozen other voices backed him.

"We did. Ask Lucas."

Lucas bobbed his head vigorously, a broad grin on his face. He knew something these smart-alecs didn't, and it tickled him to pieces.

"Lucas and I have been toting water to it." At first, Rush had worried that the stallion wouldn't drink, but thirst had overcome its hesitancy. And it had cleaned up a good portion of oats this morning. That had relieved the fear that the horse might go on a hunger strike.

95

"You don't believe me?" he challenged. "Come on and I'll show you."

Lucas hobbled along beside him, and there was a bounce in that gimpy step.

There wasn't a sound in them as they stared over the gates. And every face carried the same stamp of awe as it stared at the stallion. It snorted and raced to the far end of the canyon, and that broke the spell.

"Starshell," Yates yelled. "My God, it's him."

They packed around Rush, clamoring for every detail, and he couldn't have pried in a word with a pinch bar.

"Shut up," Lucas yelled. "Let him talk." He had heard it several times, and he still wanted to hear it again.

Rush recounted every detail, and they couldn't get enough of it.

Yates looked at him thoughtfully and said, "You're smarter than I thought you were." That was envy in his voice, but it was normal envy, and Rush didn't resent it.

"You can help me carry water to him for that," Rush said.

"Man, that'd be a pleasure. When are you going to break him?"

"I thought in the morning. I'll need some help."

That was malice in Yates' eyes. "Are you scared?"

Hell yes, Rush was scared. Starshell was a big, powerful animal. A horse like that could pile up bruises on a man.

Odie stomped into the parlor, and his face was black. Ben Cavanaugh glanced up from the paper he was reading and asked, "What's eating you?"

"That damned Rush sold a bunch of horses to the British army. I heard about it in Ontario."

Ben started to shrug it away. He didn't see anything to get steamed up over. Rush had probably sold three or four head. But Odie had said a bunch. "How many?" he asked.

Odie grinned maliciously. That disinterest wasn't fooling him any. "Sixty head."

"Where in the hell did he get that many?" his father exploded.

"The little ranchers threw in together and made a drive of the oreanas. I heard he got forty dollars a head." Ben Cavanaugh never listened to him. He had thrown his newspaper aside. He was listening now.

Ben whistled. That came to a lot of money.

"He probably got them off of our land," Odie said.

Ben considered that then shook his head. He might have, though he doubted it. Rush had an awful lot of country to run in. He'd stay off of Cavanaugh land.

Odie's face turned sullen. "Some major is buying them. I talked to him, and he's satisfied with Rush. He wants more, but he's going to let Rush deliver them."

Ben eyed his son speculatively. Odie had a greedy eye for a dollar. He was a damned fool with his money, and Ben never allowed him any. All he did with it was spend it on some dance-hall floozie. It wasn't hard to read Odie's mind. He was thinking of what a swarth he could cut with some of that horse money.

"What have you got in mind, Odie?"

Odie's face brightened. His father was willing to listen. "I was thinking we'd wait until they made their next gather, then take it away from them."

Ben stared at his son so long that Odie shifted uneasily. That silence meant Ben was building up something.

"Have you lost your goddamned head?" Ben shouted. "Counting the hands, they'd be eight altogether. If the little ranches had thrown in together, they'd amount to twenty-five or thirty men." Fury kept growing in his face. "Do you know what kind of odds we'd be facing? Or did you just plan on riding up and asking them politely to turn them over?"

Odie scrubbed the floor with his foot. His father never could see one of his ideas. "You won't be buying any more cheap land," he said. "If they can sell all the oreanas they can catch, it'll put them back on their feet."

That was a bitter pill to swallow. Ben Cavanaugh hated

to see the little ranchers get up off of the floor—particularly the Sawyers. But he didn't see anything he could do about it—except wish them bad luck for the future.

He turned his wrath on Odie. "Get out of here and let me read in peace."

A thought occured to him, and he stopped Odie at the door. "Take Burr with you and do some riding. If you see any of them on our land, shoot them for trespassing." It wasn't much, but it was all he could think of at the moment.

He scowled as Odie slammed the door. Odie was getting too big for his britches. He'd have to take him down a peg or two one of these days.

Odie found the foreman in the barn. Burr Cawley was a broad-chested, bandy-legged man with a sharp, beady eye in a hard face. He and Odie always got along well together. They had the same ideas about most things.

Cawley took a look at Odie's sour face and said, "You look like you're snake-bit."

Odie had a sympathetic ear, and he poured it all out. Cawley whistled at the amount of money that Rush had already collected.

"Maybe we could shape up our own drive," he said.

Odie shook his head. Nobody would throw in with them, and they wouldn't have enough men. The major wouldn't buy from them, and besides, Ben had already vetoed the whole idea.

"Ben wants us to do some riding to be sure none of them crosses our land." His face said how unacceptable the order was. It'd be a lot of hours in the saddle without a damned thing accomplished.

"We could keep our eyes open," Cawley said. "A man never knows what might turn up."

Odie's face brightened. Cawley was right. It made the thought of those hours in the saddle more bearable. He said, "Burr, I wish we could get our hands on some of that money."

"So do I," Cawley said fervently. "So do I."

XIII

"You TRYING to kill yourself?" Yates demanded as Rush picked himself up off the ground again.

Rush gave him a painful grin. He ached in every muscle, and he doubted he could put his finger on an unbruised spot. This was the third time Starshell had dumped him, and serious misgivings were in his mind that he would ever ride him.

He poured a dipperful of water over his head and breathed hard. Both shoulders of his shirt were burst through by scraping contact with the hard ground, and he bled a little at the mouth. He gingerly moved his tongue and found where he had bitten his lower lip.

He glanced at the far side of the corral. Starshell was caught up again, and it stood panting hard. It didn't hold its head as high, and gouts of foam dropped from its nostrils. Those three attempts at riding the animal had taken a lot out of it. Rush thought grimly, *But he's still got something left.*

Starshell didn't buck; he exploded. He had steel springs in his legs, and he went higher and came down harder than any horse Rush had ever experienced. He could land on a stiffened foreleg and snap the shock through its body until it culminated in a savage, smashing blow against the rider. He could swap ends until Rush didn't think his neck was going to be strong enough to keep his head from flying off into space. He knew every wily trick, and he had endurance and power to back them up.

"I stayed on him a little longer that time, didn't I?" Rush wanted encouragement; he needed it.

"Yeah. Maybe a half-second longer. Let me take a crack at him." Yates face was eager.

Rush shook his head. This was his horse. He was going to ride it—or nobody was.

He sighed and took a limping stride toward it.

"You'd better give yourself a little time," Yates protested.

Rush needed time to recover. He was the first to admit it. But that time would also work to the stallion's advantage. He kept on moving toward it.

"All right," Yates called after him. "I'll scrape you up off of the rocks."

Rush didn't want to put his foot into the stirrup. He wasn't even sure he could swing his leg high enough to clear the saddle. Every fiber of him screamed in protest at the coming punishment. But this was a matter of will against will, endurance against endurance. Rush hoped Starshell was weakening as much as he was.

He swung up, and hands released the horse. He looked around at the watching faces. There was no more yelling and whooping now. This had turned into too grim a battle.

Starshell stood there as though debating whether or not it was worth it to go on with this. Then he squealed and bounded into the air.

Rush groaned as he landed. Jesus, that ripped through him like red-hot knives. He locked his teeth to keep from biting himself again, and his world turned into a crazy, spinning, tilting thing. He rode an arched bow, and when it straightened, he thought it would catapult him over the canyon wall. A man lost track of time up here, for a second became an eternity. He was going to keep track of the bucks, but he lost count somewhere around a half-dozen. Up and down, up and down with each landing a hammer-blow against the base of his spine. He knew a wild rage at the horse. Didn't it ever quit?

Then suddenly it was over. It took a long moment for Rush to realize it. His world was no longer spinning and tilting. The horizon was in its proper place, and the land looked stable again. Starshell had finally concluded he couldn't dislodge that burr on its back.

The yelling broke out, loud and sustained, and Rush

grinned weakly at them. He prodded Starshell to make sure there wasn't a heave left in him, and the horse only moved wearily forward a few steps.

If Rush wasn't so damned beaten up, he would've done some yelling, too. But that would take effort he didn't have.

"Open the gates," he called.

He saw the argument on Yates' face and knew its source. If Starshell bucked outside the corral and threw him, he could lose the horse. But he didn't think it was going to buck.

He let the stallion move out at a slow walk and tensed in fearful anticipation as they passed the gates. But the fight was all gone, and Starshell was content to plod along.

Rush rode him out of the canyon. He judged he had gone a good half-mile before he turned and brought him back. The gates swung to behind him, and he stepped down.

Yates threw out a quick hand and steadied him, and Rush was grateful for it.

"I didn't think you'd ever do it," Yates said.

"That makes two of us," Rush answered.

He stripped off saddle and bridle, and while the horse cowered under his touch, it made no resistance.

"Let me carry that water," Yates said gruffly.

Rush wanted to let him. Those buckets weighed a ton; they were pulling his arms from the sockets, but he wanted no one else to wait on the stallion.

Starshell backed a few steps as Rush approached, then held. It eyed the water Rush set down before it, then came forward. It thrust its muzzle into one of the buckets. It snorted and raised its head as Rush reached out and touched it, then went back to its drinking.

"You've got him," Mundro said, and his eyes were shining.

"Yes," Rush said in simple acknowledgment. He had to bring in some oats before he could sit down and ease his trembling legs. Starshell probably wouldn't eat right now, but Rush wanted him to know he could depend on food and water from him.

He locked in the groan as he sat down. He wouldn't be able to walk for a week.

The men were filled with the battle they had seen, and Rush listened to them talk. They were as proud as though each of them had done it himself.

"He's going to be a help," Rush said. He rolled a smoke and was surprised at how good it tasted. Maybe he would recover sooner than he thought.

"He knows every canyon, every gulley where his band ranges." Rush said. "He'll take us to them." He snapped the cigarette away and was surprised at the distance he got. He did have some strength left. "We'll have to move," he went on. "It's too far to drive them here. We'll start tomorrow."

"What's another day going to hurt?" Mundro asked.

"No, we start tomorrow," Rush said firmly.

He couldn't find another box canyon, and they had to build fences on both ends of this one. He worked some of the stiffness out of him, but he couldn't do much about the bruises. Time would have to take care of that.

The work went fast. They had money in their pockets, and this would bring more.

Yates straightened and wiped the sweat from his face. "Something bothering you?" he asked. "You keep looking around."

Rush had a crawly feeling along his skin. "I feel like somebody's watching us," he confessed.

Yates scanned the horizon in all directions, and it was empty. "Are you sure he didn't scramble your brains?"

"It could be," Rush admitted. For he hadn't seen a moving thing. But the crawly feeling wouldn't go away.

He pushed it out of his mind and said, "I guess we're all set to start the drive tomorrow."

He turned and walked toward Starshell, and the horse nickered a welcome.

Rush smiled at Yates. "He gentled down real good, didn't he?"

102

"I feel real envy of you for the first time," Yates said and sighed.

Rush stroked the satiny neck. "He's going to be a help tomorrow." Yates had a right to his envy. Every horseman would feel the same thing every time he looked at this animal.

Odie and Cawley lay on a high promontory watching the drive. Odie grew more livid every passing minute. "Goddamn him," he said passionately. "He's going to make it."

The glasses were glued to his eyes as he watched the oreanas being driven ever nearer the trap. He owed Rush Sawyer something, and it galled him to see see all that money falling into his hands. Yates, too, he thought viciously. He'd like to have both of them lying on the ground so he could stomp them into pulp.

He squirmed uncomfortably on the hard ground. The leading wild horses were just disappearing into the canyon mouth. "He's got it," he said glumly. "How many do you think he picked up?"

Cawley put his glasses down. "A hell of a lot of them. Maybe close to three hundred. I'd say they cleaned up today." He sighed with regret. "And we can't do a thing about it." He rolled a cigarette and licked it. "He'd never have done it without that red stallion. Man, that's a horse."

"The bastard was always lucky," Odie said glumly. From the moment he had seen Rush astride the horse he had wanted it with an intensity that made him ache. He had never believed the legend about the horse. He had to believe it now.

"What do you think that stallion's worth?" he asked. It was idle conjecture; an answer would only add to his torture.

Cawley squinted his eyes. "He'd bring five hundred dollars in some places. Find the right buyer out of state. Say in Wyoming or Montana—" He broke off and shook his head. "Right now, I'd settle for five hundred. Because we're going to get nothing."

103

Odie's words rushed out. "The two of us can't handle that herd. But two men sure might handle one horse."

Cawley's eyes went round. "If you got the idea I think you're crazy."

"Would it hurt to look it over?" Odie asked.

A glitter started in Cawley's eyes, and he took a long, careful breath. "It wouldn't hurt to sorta look things over," he agreed.

XIV

YATES' FACE was filled with awe as he looked at the milling horses in the improvised corral.

"Rush, we're looking at ten thousand dollars on the hoof."

Rush nodded soberly. That figure wasn't too far off. Of course, split into as many shares as it had to be no one individual would get a great big amount. He denied that conclusion immediately. A few hundred dollars that a man didn't have to spend on his living could do so many things. It would be an unexpected payday for all of them, and a cattleman knew too few of those. No sir, he couldn't find a thing wrong with this.

Yates summed it all up. "And there's more out there. We might have to dig harder, and we may never grab another bunch as big as this one. It's like having one big bank account out there, and we can go and draw on it as long as we want."

That was pretty near the truth as long as Whitmore kept on buying. And Yates had said, the major wanted more just as fast as he could get them. Rush hoped he stuck to it. He'd gladly supply horses for every trooper in the British army.

He swept the horizon again with his eyes, and Yates

asked, "Is that still itching you? I kept my eyes open all day, and I didn't see a thing."

Rush hadn't either, that is nothing he could put his finger on. Once, he thought he had seen a stabbing ray of reflected light such as the sun would make if it caught a pair of glasses right. But it was gone so quickly that he had to put it down to a trick of his imagination.

"I'm going to stand guard tonight, Jim," he said in sudden decision.

Yates swore, and Rush said impatiently, "I know. I'm probably a damned fool. But I want to see those horses there in the morning."

Yates argued with him, and Rush lost his temper. "I'm not asking you to stand it."

"Just tell me what you think can happen. That's all I want to know."

"I don't know," Rush said helplessly. Probably nothing. But the loss of some sleep would be a cheap price to pay if it erased this uneasy feeling. He could move the camp to the mouth of the canyon, but he had purposely placed it some distance away to keep the man smell from further exciting the wild horses. And it was purposeless asking tired men to make additional effort on no more basis than he had. It wasn't longer than a half-hour until dark, and the men were relaxed and waiting for supper. He smiled faintly as he imagined the outraged howls, if he said, "Come on. Let's move." He had Starshell in among the oreanas, and the stallion was already exerting a soothing effect. Was he going to destroy all that because he couldn't get a wild hair out of his mind?

"Go on and eat, Jim. You might bring me something out later on."

Yates scowled, but made no comment. "Where are you going to be?"

Rush pointed to a small level spot about halfway up the canyon wall. It gave him a sweep of the approach to the canyon, but darkness would eliminate that. Then he'd have to depend on hearing and instinct.

"I'll bring you something," Yates said and strode away.

The shadows came up from the ground and blended in a great, dark arch overhead. The wind rustled the brush, and Rush started every time it scraped branches together. Maybe he was keyed up because he wanted so badly to deliver this second bunch. It was a normal night with normal night sounds.

"You're a damned fool," he told himself.

He heard the scrape of a boot before he could make out the dark bulk of a man approaching him. "Jim?" he called softly.

"Who were you expecting?" Yates jeered.

Rush eased his tight grip on the carbine. It wasn't hard for a man to work himself into a nervous state.

Yates brought a plate of food and pot of coffee and a tin cup. "I spilled some of it," he said. "I tripped and fell. It's so damned black a man can't see a foot in front of him. Lucas was slower than ever tonight. I been waiting all this time on him."

He was silent until Rush finished eating, then he asked, "Seen any ghosts yet?"

"Not a one. And I hope it keeps that way."

"I'll be out about midnight and relieve you."

"Did I ask you to?"

"Don't get huffy with me," Yates said. "I got a right to make as big a fool out of myself as you have."

"I'll let you kick my ass in the morning, Jim."

"And I might do just that," Yates growled before he turned away.

Rush shook his head. This job wasn't of Yates' making, but he was willing to share it. If Yates wanted that kick in the morning, Rush would stand still for it.

Night hours moved slowly. Rush shifted his position time after time, and there were no soft spots. He stood and moved a few feet to ease his cramped position. When Yates came out to relieve him, he was going to be damned grateful.

He jumped as a voice came out of the blackness. "Rush?"

"Here, Jim," he replied.

Yates materialized out of the darkness. "Go get some sleep," he said. He could see no necessity in this, and he was half angry. "And don't think I'm not going to collect in the morning."

"You just keep awake," Rush said. He grinned as Yates' swearing followed him down the hill.

The night was cool, but Odie was sweating. He had removed his boots, and his feet were bruised and sore. He had marked Rush's position well before dark, and he had worked his way a careful inch at a time down the slope. He couldn't talk Cawley into doing this. Cawley had said, "It's your show. You do it."

Odie put vengeful thoughts against the man. If he got Starshell out of the corral, maybe he'd cut Cawley out entirely. He had it coming.

But first he had to locate Rush's exact position, and this damned blackness was like trying to peer through a brick wall.

He froze as a tiny flame flared into life. It wasn't twenty feet ahead of him. He stood motionless as he saw the wink of the cigarette as it sucked fire from the match. That winking red eye placed Rush for him. Now it was only a matter of covering the remaining distance unheard and unseen. He had picked a late hour, an hour when a man's vitality was at its lowest. He suspected Rush had lit that cigarette to help him keep awake.

He eased the pistol from its holster and moved forward a fraction at a time. He was so tense his muscles ached, and surely, Rush must hear the thumping of his heart.

The cigarette arced away and landed in a shower of sparks. He no longer had his beacon, but he didn't need it. He was less than six feet behind his victim.

Some instinct must have warned Rush, for he swiveled his head about. A bulky shadow leaped out of the night, and an arm brought the pistol barrel down with savage ferocity.

107

Odie breathed hard as he stared at the crumpled form. He felt limp after the tension. By God, he'd done it, and elation swelled within him. He was even with Rush Sawyer. In a burst of senseless rage, he struck again at the unprotected head, then toed the form over. It flopped with a grotesque sprawl of arms and legs that told him Rush was dead.

But he bent close to make sure and sucked in his breath sharply at the discovery. He had killed Jim Yates. He argued himself out of his disappointment. Wasn't this just as good? Didn't he owe Yates something, too?

He straightened and listened, and the night was quiet. A slight change of plans occurred to him, and he grinned. People might grieve over the accident, but not a finger would point at him.

He grabbed Yates under the armpits, then dragged him down the hill. He let the body flop in front of the corral gates and said a cautious, "Burr."

Cawley appeared from the opposite side and squatted to look at the dead man. "Hell, that's not Sawyer."

"I know who it is. Shut up and listen to me."

They would go into the corral and get a rope on the stallion. That would take some doing, but everything had gone all right so far. After Starshell was led out of the corral they would leave the gates open. They wouldn't have to drive the oreanas out. They would find the opened gate and stampede through it in their eagerness to get away. After all those horses ran over the body nobody could say he wasn't killed by them. As for Starshell it would look as though he had escaped with the others.

"You really got it figured, Odie," Cawley said admiringly.

Odie swelled with pride. Ben never gave him any credit for brains. He wished he could tell his father about this. He had wiped out the beating Yates and given him and undid Rush's hard work. He'd say it was one hell of a night.

XV

THE HARD drumming of hooves jerked Rush out of deep sleep. For a moment he had the impression he lay directly in the path of a stampede. He listened, and the sound was too far away for it to be coming at him.

The oreanas! He didn't see how it was possible, but in some manner, they had forced open the corral gates. Probably in milling around, a mass of them had put pressure on the gates and they had given.

He yelled and jumped to his feet, and all around him sleepy men came out of their blankets. "The oreanas," he yelled. "They're out." Yates would be trying to stop them, and he would be helpless.

He sat down and tugged on his boots, cursing their stubbornness. But he couldn't make much time in his sock feet.

He got them on and ran as hard as he could, and he heard the others pounding behind him. By the time he reached the canyon, the oreanas were gone, their hoofbeats only a faint echo.

His shoulders drooped in dejection. He thought of all the things they should have done, and it was a waste. It was too late to think of making those gates more secure now.

The others joined him, and their reactions were varied. Some cursed in wild anger, and others stood silent under the enormity of their loss.

Rush remembered that Yates was around here some place, and he called, "Jim, where are you?"

He called again and got no response. Surely, Yates hadn't tried to run after the horses on foot.

"Scatter out. Find Jim," he said and walked toward the gates. He almost stumbled over the still form, and something tight blocked his throat making each breath a tearing, painful thing.

He stooped and lit a match, and the sight of that battered figure wrung a cry of distress from him. He could read what had happened. Yates had tried to block the escape of the oreanas, and they had stampeded over him.

He squatted on his heels for a long time and knew the kind of silent grief that racked a man. Mundro put his hand on his shoulder, and Rush didn't feel its touch.

He kept staring at that broken form, and he felt the awkward, unspoken sympathy all around him. Everybody here knew how close Jim Yates and Rush had been.

"What'll we do, boy?" Mundro asked, and it broke the frozen trance.

"Carry him back to camp," he said, managing to find the words in the void of his mind.

He walked to the corral gates wanting anything to relieve his mind from thinking about Jim. He stared at them a long time before he realized he was seeing something. Those gates should have been twisted and battered to the ground. A herd of horses, if their weight had torn them loose, would have left a tangled mess. And the gates were intact, just swung wide.

Something nebulous was trying to take shape in his mind, and right now, he couldn't give it help. He lit several matches hunting along the ground and came up with pieces of wire. There were the wires that bound the gates together, and human fingers had to untwist them.

"What is it?" Mundro asked, a puzzled frown on his face.

"I don't know yet," Rush said. That nebulous something was taking a vague form, but it was still fuzzy around the edges. "I'll join you later," he said, not realizing how short his words were.

He walked to the spot where Yates had relieved him, and felt around with his hands. He touched Yates' carbine and picked it up. His eyes were hard as he stared into space. Now, that something was taking definite form in his head. Yates would have carried his carbine with him.

He walked back to camp and kept his eyes off the blanket-ed form. "Take him in to Doc Somers in the morning," he said. "Tell Doc to make a thorough examination."

He refused the questions asked him and sat down by himself. The rest of them respected his want of privacy, and he listened to the subdued murmur of their talk. Lucas built up the fire and made coffee.

Rush turned down a cup, and Lucas said, "Damnit, Rush. I know—" He looked at that bleak face, shook his head, and turned away.

Rush was in the saddle at day's first light. He looked down at his father and said, "I'll join you in town, later." Something besides an accident had happened, and he needed a few more pieces of sustaining evidence.

He went first to the little bench where he had last seen Yates. The ground from there to the spot before the corral gates was hard and mostly rocky, but he found several scratches in the scattered patches of earth that would take an impression. A man's bootheels if he were dragged by the arms would make such scratches.

It was well in the afternoon before he found Starshell's bunch of oreanas. He lay atop a ridge watching them through his glasses. He had no doubt that was the same bunch. He remembered that byo with its outstanding mark-ings and that palamino mare that towered over the others in size. And the numbers of this bunch were about right. But Starshell wasn't with them. And he would be if he had escaped with them last night.

When he arose, his face was a granite mask. He had enough answers to suit him. And if they didn't suit Sam Tabor, to hell with him.

He walked into Doc Somers' office an hour before sunset. Somers shook his head in regret and said, "A terrible thing, Rush."

"Yes," Rush answered curtly. "Did you examine him?"

"As well as I could, Rush. All those hooves—" He shook his head and didn't finish.

111

Rush knew a vast disappointment. He had expected Somers to be afire with something he had found.

"You didn't find anything unusual?"

Somers frowned. "There was something, Rush. It's been troubling me ever since I discovered it."

"What is it?" Rush asked harshly.

"His head was broken over the ear. A long, narrow depression."

"Like a pistol barrel might make?"

"It's pure guesswork, Rush. A hoof—"

"Wouldn't make the same kind of break. And it's been on your mind ever since you found it. Come on."

"Where?" Somers asked.

"To Tabor's office." He said impatiently at Somers' hesitance, "I just want you to tell him what you've told me. I'm not asking you to swear to anything."

Tabor looked up from his desk as they entered. "I'm sorry, Rush," and he meant it. "He could make a man so damned mad, but there wasn't any malice in him."

Rush nodded. He wasn't here to talk about Yates—at least, not directly.

"Tell him, Doc," he ordered.

Somers frowned as he talked. He finished and said, "In any other circumstances I might say he was struck over the ear with a pistol barrel."

Tabor listened attentively. "Go on," he said softly.

Somers shrugged. "But with so many hooves striking him—"

"That's all, Doc," Rush said. "I'll let you know if I need you any more." He worked Somers toward the door.

He came back, and Tabor asked crossly, "What was that all about?"

"Will you listen?"

Tabor searched his face, then nodded.

Rush told him about his unease and of the events leading up to the time Yates relieved him at guard duty. "I heard the hoofbeats and thought the oreanas had busted

112

out. Jim was lying right in front of the gates, and they'd run over him."

"Mundro told me all that," Tabor said impatiently.

"But the corral gates weren't smashed to pieces. They were just standing open." He pulled some coiled pieces of wire from his pocket. "The gates were tied with these. They were straight when I found them. I coiled them to carry them."

The frown disappeared from Tabor's face, and his eyes were more intent.

"I found Jim's carbine where he'd been sitting. And that was quite a piece from the gates."

"He could've dropped it when he ran to stop them from breaking out."

Rush glared at him. "Are you throwing out the gates?"

"No," Tabor muttered.

"I found marks where he'd been dragged. They led right to where he was lying."

"What are you trying to say?" Tabor demanded.

"You heard I'd captured Starshell?"

"Yes, and I'm damned sorry he got away."

"Maybe he didn't get away. Maybe he was stolen."

"Of all the crazy ideas," Tabor exploded.

"Listen to me," Rush yelled. "I found his band, and he wasn't with them. Wouldn't he have been, if he'd escaped with them?"

Tabor took a careful breath. "You're saying—"

"I'm saying Jim was murdered, then dragged to where the oreanas could run over him. It made a perfect cover-up except whoever did it left a lot of untied strings."

"I guess next you'll name the man," Tabor snorted.

"I think I can," Rush steadily. "I think it was meant for me." His face twisted briefly. "And Jim got it instead. I can name one man who hated both of us enough to do it."

Tabor's voice lowered until it was little more than a whisper. "Are you saying Odie Cavanaugh—"

"Odie Cavanaugh," Rush repeated.

"You're crazy," Tabor yelled. "You haven't got a shred of

113

proof that would stand up in court. A judge would throw you out before he listened to your third wild guess."

"Sam, you never saw a horse like Starshell. Anybody who saw him would want him. I don't think Odie could let go of him."

Tabor's eyes were round. "Are you saying Odie's got the horse hidden somewhere? Maybe at the ranch?"

"That's it, Sam. I'm asking for your help. And if you don't go with me, I'll look anyway."

Tabor gave it long consideration. "You know you could get your head blown off? And Ben would be within his rights."

Rush's eyes never wavered.

"If you can't find the horse, you'll drop this?"

Rush finally nodded. He'd have to.

Tabor heaved himself out of his chair. "I guess I got a right to be as big a damned fool as you have."

Once again, Rush's face twisted. Jim Yates had said exactly the same words to him.

XVI

BEN CAVANAUGH awakened from a fitful sleep. He had the feeling it was very late even before he struck a match and looked at his watch. It was after three in the morning, and he cursed with the petulance of a man groggy with sleep. If Odie was in by now, he was going to have his hide. He had checked four times before, and Odie hadn't been in his room. Odie was doing a lot of late riding these last few days, and when questioned about it, turned sullen and secretive. Ben was sure he knew what that riding was about. Odie still had those wild horses in mind. Ben knew his youngest son well. Once, he got an idea in his head, nothing could drag it out. He was going to get that head blown off if he messed around Rush Sawyer's horses.

The thought brought terror to Ben. He raved at Odie's deficiencies, but Odie was still all he had. If something happened to Odie, he would be left a lonely, old man, and he never could face that thought squarely.

He looked into Odie's room, and it was empty. He swore passionately. The next time he told Odie to stay away from Sawyer he'd make it so plain that even Odie would understand.

He didn't feel like going back to bed, and he prowled the house restlessly. He paused at every window and looked out over his land. He was suddenly depressed and weary. A man struggled all his life to amass something, and there was no satisfaction in it at the end.

He stiffened as he saw dark figures of two horsemen turn the corner of the barn and approach its door. They were leading a third horse. His anger was so great that he thought it would choke him. Had Odie been damn fool enough to steal a single horse from Sawyer? From the furtive movements of the two riders, he would say it was likely.

He watched them disappear into the barn, then hurried into his room to dress. He tugged on his boots, then hastened out of the house.

They were still in the barn. He could hear them talking in hushed tones as he stepped through the door. They were arguing about where to put a horse, and he got within a few feet of them before he spoke.

"What the hell do you think you're doing?" he roared.

Odie made a frightened squeak, and Cawley muttered an oath under his breath.

"Nothing, Pa," Odie said. "Burr and I ran this stallion down this afternoon. We were just talking about which stall to put him in."

"Light the lantern," Ben ordered.

Odie stood strangely hesitant, and Ben yelled, "Move."

Odie took the lantern down from its nail and lit it. Its light pushed the shadow back into the corners of the barn.

115

Ben stared open-mouthed at the horse. He had seen a lot of horses in his life but nothing like this one. Just looking at it made him weak. He ran his tongue around in a dry mouth before he could speak. "Is that Starshell?" he demanded. He had always scoffed at the legend as being the product of some drunken cowhand's imagination. Even now, with his eyes filled with the animal, he could hardly believe it.

"Yes," Odie muttered.

"You and Burr didn't run him down," Ben said scornfully. "I want the truth." His voice lowered to a quiet, ominous note. "Don't try to lie to me."

Odie's eyes were filled with defiance, then he caved in suddenly. His mind couldn't fasten on a fitting lie fast enough, and if it did, he knew it wouldn't stand. Ben always knew when he was lying.

He told Ben exactly how it had happened and finished by saying, "I thought it was Rush instead of Yates."

Ben's only regret was that it hadn't been Rush. His eyes glittered as he looked at the horse. At that, Odie had been pretty cute about it. Nobody could ever say Yates hadn't died under the trampling hooves of the oreanas.

"What did you think you were going to do with him?" he growled.

Odie made a helpless gesture. "I thought we'd get him out of the country and sell him. He ought to bring five hundred dollars."

Easily, Ben agreed. He'd give that much for the horse, himself. Odie could never think anything through to its conclusion. He couldn't make the horse invisible, and everybody who saw the horse would talk about it. And some of that talk would be sure to drift back to Rush. Night traveling would minimize the danger but wouldn't eliminate it entirely. And if Rush got the slightest inkling of what happened to Starshell, Odie was a dead man.

It was on Ben's tongue to say, *Turn him loose,* but he couldn't get the words out. My God, to have a horse like

116

this in his hands, then have to turn it loose— His spirit groaned in agony at the thought.

He'd give half of his remaining life to have some foals by this stallion. He thought of some of the mares he owned. If they were covered by Starshell— The thought put a giddy roaring in his ears. The resultant product would be more than the talk of the county. The whole state would hear about it. Hell, he could go farther than that. They'd be coming to him from all over the west trying to buy one of them.

"We'll keep him," he said abruptly.

Cawley threw him an alarmed glance, and Odie made that frightened squeak again.

Ben knew both of them were thinking of the danger, and he admitted it was there. But goddamnit, this was Cavanaugh land, and nobody came on it without his permission. They could keep Starshell hidden until at least some of his best mares were bred. So far, only the three of them knew about it, and it would be a problem to keep it from the hands. But it could be done. If he waited until the hands were out before he brought a mare to Starshell, he could hide the stallion for weeks. He made his decision. He was going to try it.

"Pa—" Odie started.

Ben put those cold eyes on him, and Odie's protest died. He looked at Cawley and said, "If this gets out, Burr, I know where to look."

Cawley shifted uneasily. He had always been afraid of the old man.

"I'll give you one of his first foals," Ben promised in a reckless burst of generosity. "You, too, Odie."

He was satisfied with the gleam that came into their eyes. That would hold them. It would hold any man.

He put some thought on where he could conceal the stallion. The stalls were out. Anybody, stepping into the barn, would spot him immediately. He thought of the old grain bin. It was big enough to hold the horse, and its door fit right, against leakage of grain, until it took a sharp eye to trace its fine crack. It might not do for the long run, but it would do fine for now.

He led the stallion toward it, and the animal followed docilely. It filled him with wicked glee. Rush had done a fine job in breaking him.

He put Starshell into the bin, and he had ample room. "Feed and water him," he said, before he turned away. He could see a lot of problems ahead, but a man had to be prepared to risk much, if he wanted to gain much.

He strode back to the house, his head busy with thoughts. Maybe he'd better send the crew, all except Cawley, to clean up and repair the line shacks. The timing of the order might come as a surprise to them, but they wouldn't question it. And with them out of the way for a prolonged spell, it'd give him breathing room. He could come up with something better than the bin for the stallion. He grinned wolfishly. This was going to be the biggest night of his life.

At the end of the next day, some of the tenseness left Ben Cavanaugh. If Rush had had any suspicions at all, he would have hot-tailed it out here. No, Rush thought his horse was out running with the oreanas in the breaks.

"How did I get myself talked into this?" Tabor asked glumly as he trudged toward the Cavanaugh buildings. They couldn't just ride up to the house, and they had left their horses well behind them.

"Because it adds up to the same for you as it does for me," Rush snapped.

If they were discovered, they were in an awkward position, Tabor thought. They couldn't make a run for it, and they'd be lucky if Cavanaugh and his hands didn't shoot first and ask for identities second. There was something about sulking shadows on a man's land at night that made him nervous.

"If we don't find the horse, Rush, what then?"

Rush took so long with his answer that Tabor said, "Well?"

"I'd have to give it up," Rush said quietly. "I'd say Odie had gotten him away somehow. I wouldn't stop my believing.

I'd just have to stop looking." And that would only be because he didn't know where to turn.

"Okay," Tabor said gruffly. He felt he should add something, and he said, "We'll give it the best look we can tonight."

The moon would be up in another hour, but now the night was dark. The buildings first came into view as darker blobs against a lighter background. They made a semi-circle, observing the buildings from several angles. The bunkhouse was dark, and that was a little unusual, for it wasn't that late. Still, Rush had known many a tired cowhand to go to bed with the last light of day.

A light was on in the house, and Tabor grunted, "It's coming from the parlor. I think Ben lost all his dogs."

They went in slow and easy checking out the bunkhouse first. Rush went one way, Tabor the other. Rush paused at each window, and he heard no sound of snoring. He met Tabor, and Tabor said, "I think it's empty."

Rush nodded. It had that feel to him, too.

He hesitated at the door before he stepped inside. He moved the length of the structure, and not a bunk was occupied. He came back and said, "Ben must've sent them someplace."

"Good," Tabor murmured. "We won't have to worry about them."

They found no horses in the corral attached to the barn, and Rush scowled at that. Usually, a man's personal mount was kept handy. This empty corral said the Cavanaughs would have to do some walking to catch up their horses.

"Damned odd," he said, and Torbor grunted his response.

They slipped into the barn, and Tabor stayed near the door, keeping an eye on the house. Rush went up and down the runways, and every stall was empty. The pungent aroma of manure, both old and new, filled his nostrils. He made the rounds again, and his desperation was mounting.

Tabor came back from the doorway and said, "You're taking long enough."

119

"Give me a few minutes longer, Sam. He's got to be in here."

"Ah," Tabor said in quiet understanding. "You wanted it so bad you're just hoping, Rush. We've done everything we could."

Rush heaved a heavy sigh. He had been so positive he had figured this out. He guessed Tabor was right. He had wanted it so badly that his imagination could take over.

He started to move, and he heard a small, muted thump such as a horse might make in restless stirring: not a kick, put a picking up and putting down of a hoof.

He gripped Tabor's arm and asked tensely, "Did you hear that?"

Tabor listened. "I don't hear anything," he said irritably. "Damn it, Rush, you've worked yourself up so much—" He broke off as a thump carried to him. He jerked his head toward Rush. "Is that what you heard?"

Rush nodded. "A horse standing on a wooden floor might make that kind of thump."

"But where in the hell is he?" Tabor asked in exasperation. "That's a blank wall in front of us."

Rush stepped forward and ran his hands carefully over the wall. He found a tiny crack in the dovetailed boards and ran his fingers along it. It outlined a door.

"Come here, Sam." New hope made his voice husky.

Tabor traced the door crack with his fingers. He pried at it, and nothing moved. "I wish we had a light," he muttered.

"I bumped into a lantern back there," Rush said. "I'm going to get it and close the barn door."

"Damned risky," Tabor muttered. But he didn't say no.

Rush shuddered as the door groaned dismally. It seemed to him that the sound carried twenty miles. He waited a long time and saw no activity starting from the house. He finished closing the door and came back and got the lantern. He picked up a horse blanket to shield its light and said, "See if it's a door, Sam."

It was a door all right, and no wonder they couldn't pry it open with their fingers. It was wedged tight with three small pegs wedged in at the bottom. Tabor kicked them loose, and the door swung open. A hot wave of horse smell flowed through the door, wrapping about them.

"Move the lantern closer," Tabor said, and his voice wasn't steady.

Rush moved a step closer and held up the lantern. Its light flooded the room, and Starshell snorted and moved back against the far wall.

Tabor stared at him so long that Rush thought he had lost his voice. Then Tabor said, "So that's Starshell. I never thought I'd see him this close up. I think we can go on to the house." He closed the door as Rush blew out the lantern.

Two drifting shadows crossed the yard and approached the front window. Tabor stopped at the edge of the porch. Rush stepped up on it and tested each board for creakiness before he put his weight on it. He flattened against the side of the window and removed his hat. Then crouching, he moved his head enough so that he could see into the room with one eye.

He went back with the same care and joined Tabor. "Ben and Odie and Cawley. Ben is sitting near the far wall. Odie is leaning on the fireplace, and Cawley is diagonally across from him."

"Are they armed?" Tabor whispered.

"Odie and Cawley are. Ben's sitting beneath a rifle on the wall."

"If we go in fast enough, we may catch them by surprise so they won't even think of putting up a fight."

"And if they do?" Rush asked.

Tabor snorted. "If you don't know what to do then, it's too damned late for me to be telling you."

Rush gave him a feral grin. "I'll go in first." He drew his pistol before he stepped up onto the porch again. This time he listened beside the door, and the rumble of conversation sounded normal and unalarmed.

He threw the door open and bounded inside. "Hold it," he yelled. "Move and you're dead." The ferocity in his eyes and the drawn gun were equal restraining factors. He heard Tabor come through the door on his heels, but he didn't take his eyes off Odie and Cawley. Their faces were almost ludicrous with stupefaction, and it looked as though their jaw hinges had broken, letting the lower jaw dangle.

"What the hell is this?" Ben Cavanaugh roared and started to get up.

"Sit where you are," Tabor snapped.

"Goddamnit," Ben raved. "If you think you can bust into a man's house like this—"

"Stop it," Tabor said wearily.

Rush watched Odie's face. Some guilt must be working in him for it was draining the blood from his face. Not a word of accusation had been made, but Odie knew.

Ben opened his mouth, and Tabor yelled, "I said shut up. We found Starshell in the barn."

A hard blow on the head wouldn't have stunned them more. Odie was the only one who made a sound, and it was animal-like with its anguish.

"You hit Jim over the head, Odie," Rush said savagely. "Then dragged him where the oreanas could run over him after you opened the gates. You took Starshell. And you're going to hang for it."

The word "hang" galvanized Cawley into speech. "I'm not going to hang for something you did," he shouted.

"Shut up," Ben Cavanaugh roared.

But Cawley couldn't be shut up. He was panting hard with his fear. "I thought we were just going to steal a horse. I never figured on murder."

Cawley had caved in, and Rush put his attention on Odie. "Well, Odie?" he said. He remembered the way of Yates' dying, and he didn't want Odie to quit. He wanted Odie to draw.

An insane wildness was in Odie's eyes, but his face had firmed. The threat of a drawn gun on him wasn't enough to outweigh the threat of what lay ahead of him.

Tabor thought of trying to stop it. It was in his face, then it faded. Rush and Yates had both earned it.

"No, Odie," Ben shouted.

Odie gave no indication he even heard. He clawed for his gun, and his desperate haste made it an awkward, unskilled motion. Rush waited until the gun was sliding from its holster before he drew and shot. The bullet slammed into Odie's breastbone, knocking him back against the stone-facing of the fireplace. He hung there, his eyes bulging with shock and horror. He still struggled to pull his gun, but his fingers didn't have enough strength to lift it.

Rush shot him again, squarely between the eyes, and maybe that one was for Jim. He watched Odie spin, then pitch heavily to the floor, and there was no remorse in his eyes.

Ben Cavanaugh looked at his son as though he was trying to reject an idea that had to be admitted. Both of his boys were dead, and the man who was responsible for it was still on his feet.

"You killed them both," he screamed and bounded to his feet. He clawed at the rifle on its pegs in the wall, and Tabor shouted, "Hold it, Ben."

But Ben Cavanaugh was beyond reason. He lifted the rifle and was turning, when Tabor shot. He hit him in the right elbow, and Ben dropped the rifle.

It was odd how unimportant things hit a man's mind in a moment of stress. Rush heard the rifle's clatter against the floor as vividly as though it were the only sound in the world.

Ben staggered back, gripping his shattered elbow. His face registered shock, but there was still a determination in it. He even leaned over to try to pick up the rifle.

Tabor cursed him with passionate intensity. "Do you want me to break your other arm?"

It got through to Ben, or maybe it was the pain that kicked his legs out from under him, for he slid down the wall and sat at the base of it, his head hanging low, his breathing hard and raspy.

Cawley looked at the two guns swung on him, and mortal fear turned his face washy. "Don't," he begged. "I said I was out of this. Look." His fingers carefully unbuckled his gunbelt, and it thumped to the floor.

"See what you can do for him," Tabor ordered, jerking his gun toward Ben Cavanaugh.

Cawley made a quick examination, and Ben cursed him with every breath. "It's shattered all to hell," Cawley said in awe.

"Bind it up until we can get him in to a doctor," Tabor said.

He looked at Rush, and his smile was strained. "I guess it's all wrapped up. I'll hold him here, if you'll bring in the horses."

Rush nodded. He could find a saddle in the barn and put it on Starshell. It wouldn't take long to bring in the other two horses. One of them would have to carry double, but they'd get everybody to town.

He stopped at the door for a final look. Ben Cavanaugh and Cawley would do time. Even if a judge was lenient on Ben because of his age, his remaining years would be bitterly sad. A crippled, old man had only the past to look at, and when that was all he had he might as well be dead.

He turned and ran toward the barn wanting to get this over with as quickly as possible. He had things to do. He had to ride to Ontario and tell Whitmore what happened to cause the delay. And he wanted to see Julia. Then he would return and gather up the oreanas again. Jim Yates would have approved of that. He hated a job undone. Rush could almost imagine he could see Jim's grin.

Ernest Haycox

13D

The World of John Macklin

Brotherhood of the Strange   95c

Caraven of the Occult $1.25

Dwellers in Darkness   95c

Enigma of the Unknown   95c

A Look Through Secret Doors $1.25

Strange Encounters $1.25

Orbits of the Unknown   75c

Other Dimensions   75c

Out of This World   75c

Passport to the Unknown   75c

The Strange and the Uncanny   95c

Available wherever paperbacks are sold or use this coupon.

L.P. HOLMES

The Hardest Man in the Sierra's   95c

Maverick Star   95c

Rawhide Creek   95c

The Savage Hours   75c

Ray Hogan

Guns Along the Jicarilla   75c

Killer's Gun   95c

Roxie Raker ·   95c

Showdown at Texas Flat   60c

The Wolver   60c

Available wherever paperbacks are sold or use this coupon.

GILES A. LUTZ

95c each

The Black Day

Blind Trail

The Challenger

The Deadly Deputy

Deadly Like a .45

The Demanding Land

Gun Rich

Law of the Trigger

The Lonely Ride

Man on the Run

My Brothers Keeper

The Trouble Borrower

The Vengeance Ghost

Wild Runs the River

The Wild Quarry
